Robert S. Mac Arthur

Divine Balustrades and Other Sermons

Robert S. Mac Arthur

Divine Balustrades and Other Sermons

ISBN/EAN: 9783337289898

Printed in Europe, USA, Canada, Australia, Japan

Cover: Foto ©Andreas Hilbeck / pixelio.de

More available books at **www.hansebooks.com**

Divine Balustrades

AND OTHER SERMONS

ROBERT S. MacARTHUR, D.D.

———————

FLEMING H. REVELL COMPANY

NEW YORK | CHICAGO
30 Union Square, East | 148–150 Madison Street

Publishers of Evangelical Literature

PREFACE.

IT will be noticed that some of the sermons in this volume are textual, some are topical, and some combine both these methods; while others are expository, others what are generally known as Bible readings, and still others were propared in the atmosphere of recent biblical criticism. They are sent forth with the hope and prayer that they may contribute something to the honor of the Word of God, to the salvation of men, and to the glory of Jesus Christ.

ROBERT S. MACARTHUR.

CALVARY BAPTIST STUDY,
    NEW YORK CITY.

CONTENTS.

I.

Divine Balustrades.

(PART I.)

" When thou buildest a new house, then thou shalt make a battlement for thy roof, that thou bring not blood upon thine house if any man fall from thence."—DEUT. xxii. 8.

YOU will observe that in this immediate connection we have a series of laws taking cognizance of many details of daily life. Cattle that had strayed were to be brought back; lost goods to be restored; fallen cattle to be helped; the distinction between the sexes, as indicated by their apparel, to be maintained; and in taking a bird's nest the mother-bird was to have her liberty. Our Saviour probably had this law in mind when he made his tender and beautiful allusion to God's notice of the sparrow's fall. God thus commends the spirit of kindness and mercy toward all his creatures. The man who is guilty of cruelty toward a sparrow would in favorable circumstances show a like cruelty to his brother men.

Then comes instruction in regard to the roofs of houses; care must be taken to make them safe. We are familiar with the fact that houses in the East were built with flat roofs. To a considerable degree the family lived on the roof; there they walked to enjoy the fresh air; there they met for social converse; there they often slept; there, too, they went at certain times for meditation and prayer. So it was of the utmost importance that roofs be protected, and we learn from this law that they were to be surrounded with a battlement or balustrade to make them safe. If it were not built and any one fell off, the owner by his neglect brought blood upon his house. If it were built, and one through his own carelessness fell, his blood must be on his own head, and the owner would be free from all blame. The spirit of this law, we are told, was extended to wells, bridges, and indeed to everything which might endanger life. Life is thus seen to be precious in God's sight.

We are all builders; and it is of the greatest moment that we build aright. Care must be taken with the foundation; a defect in its lowest stone may reveal itself in a crack in the highest tower. Care must be taken with the material and manner of the structure; the apostle reminds us that every man must take heed how he builds even on the sure foundation. When the house is roofed, the roof itself is to be made safe. Builders of character, builders of families, builders of society, I urge you to put balustrades on the roof of the structures you are erecting. You ought to live much on the roof; it will give you broad and heavenward views. There God's breezes will refresh you; there God's sunlight will kiss you. The roof may be the most attractive, and it may also be the most dangerous place. Guard it well. There are four balustrades to which I wish especially to call your attention, one for each side of your house.

THE SABBATH BALUSTRADE.

1 . Throw around it the balustrade of the Christian Sabbath. I use this combination of the words designedly. A reference to the meaning of the word Sabbath, and its relation to our dispensation, will justify this use of the terms.

This balustrade is a very old one. Kingdoms have risen and fallen; empires have bloomed and withered; republics "have danced into light, and died into the shade," but the Sabbath has remained. Before the days of Rome and Athens, before Babylon and Nineveh, before the royal tombs of Thebes and the mighty pyramids of Egypt, the Sabbath was. And after the gnawing tooth of time shall have crumbled them to dust, the Sabbath shall be. In the very dawn of time's morning this balustrade was erected by the mighty and gentle hand of God. Two institutions of to-day have come down to us beautiful with the innocence and radiant with the glory of Eden—the Sabbath and marriage. They withstood the Fall and all its sad consequences; they have outlived all the upheavals of society, and all the cataclysms of time. They are absolutely essential to the highest good of the race; on the Sabbath stands the glorious structure of the religious life, and on marriage the security and happiness of social life. Any theory of social life which lifts a rude and unholy hand against the sanctity and glory of marriage is to be received with the utmost detestation. You can usually judge the spirit and tendencies of any social theory by its attitude toward the marriage relation. This is often one of the best tests to be applied; it is oftenest at this point that some of the modern social theories reveal their wicked animus. Not less true is it of any system of opposition to the Sabbath. The man who strikes at either, strikes at much that is holiest in the best men and women, and also at much that is dearest to God. Palsied be the hand that would tear down this old balustrade—the Sabbath of God!

This is a balustrade which has received in marvellous ways the sanction of God. Its observance is enforced in the general Mosaic code, and afterward with all the solemnities of the decalogue. We find the first reference to the Sabbath in the second chapter of Genesis, in connection with the close of the record of creation. In some respect the reference is the more impressive because the Sabbath is not there mentioned by name. On that day God rested; he took pleasure in the work of his hand; that day he blessed, sanctified and consecrated. Are not they right who hold that its institution is as ancient, and its obligation as universal, as the race? When we go to the sixteenth chapter of Exodus we find that the observance of the Sabbath is one of the recognized institutions of the time; on that day no manna fell. There is nothing in this connection to intimate that the Sabbath was now first given; it is uniformly spoken of as something well known. Thus there was a recognition of the Sabbath not only before the giving of the law on Mount Sinai, but also, it seems, before Israel came out of Egypt. If this were the first mention of the day, how could Moses have understood God, and how could the people so readily have understood Moses? Already the keeping of the Sabbath was the "good old way." Soon after this it was re-enacted, written by the finger of God as the fourth commandment on the tables of stone, amid all the solemnities of the giving of the law. The injunction in the fourth commandment, "Remember the Sabbath day," indicates its previous ob-

servance.   There are several other hints as to its pre-
Mosaic origin; but, of course, I cannot this morning
go at length into the discussion.   It is sufficient to
remember that the fourth commandment formed a
part of the decalogue, and that the decalogue had an
authority peculiarly its own; that the New Testament does not repeal it; and that it was not for Jews
alone, but is needful to and is binding on all men
in all ages and climes.   As Dr. Adam Clarke has
said, "Thus we find, that when God finished his
creation, he instituted the Sabbath; that when he
brought the people out of Egypt he insisted on the
strict observance of it; and that when he gave
the law he made it a tenth part of the whole; such
importance has this institution in the eyes of the Supreme Being!"   As time progressed, the Sabbath
was held by the devout not in less, but in greater,
reverence.   Isaiah utters his solemn protest against
profaning it; and he also pronounces many blessings
on the proper observance of the day.   Thus he
speaks, 58th chap., 13th and 14th verses: "If thou
turn away thy foot from the Sabbath, from doing
thy pleasure on my holy day; and call the Sabbath a
delight, the holy of the Lord, honorable; and shalt
honor him, not doing thine own ways, nor finding
thine own pleasure, nor speaking thine own words;
then shalt thou delight thyself in the Lord; and I
will cause thee to ride upon the high places of the

earth, and feed thee with the heritage of Jacob, thy
father: for the mouth of the Lord hath spoken it."
These are fitting words for to-day. The Sabbath-
breakers of to-day ought to hear and heed them.
Their special form of Sabbath-breaking is in turning
their feet away from God's house, doing their own
ways, speaking their own words and finding their
own pleasure. God will not hold them guiltless who
profane his holy day. Ezekiel also makes the pro-
fanation of the day foremost among the sins of the
Jews during their time of declension. Their return to God's favor, and the revival of national prosperity, were always marked by a regard for the
Sabbath. Has the fourth commandment been abro-
gated? If so, by whom? If so, where? Christ
came not to destroy the law, but to fulfil it. True,
in fulfilling it he defined it; but he made it the more
binding. Who dare blot out the command which
the finger of God has written in the imperishable
stone! The old promise is still true—the nations
which observe the Sabbath shall ride upon the high
places of the earth. England and America, as nations, are Sabbath-keepers. England and America
side by side march up the heights of national greatness. In the noblest elements of the highest civilization they lead the world. "Woe worth the day," if it
shall ever come, when the Sabbath-breaking element
in these nations shall triumph! Then their glory

will be departed indeed, and the banner of their
splendor will be trailed in the dust; but in the strength
of our God we believe that day will never dawn.

The Sabbath with its respite from labor is an unspeakable boon to men. The law of God in the human body is in harmony with the law of God in the
divine book. It has been abundantly proved by
many actual tests, that man and beast will accomplish more in a year by working six days than seven.
Mindful of this, some heathen nations set apart a
seventh part of the time, and even called it a holy
day. I look with sorrow on the tendencies to secu-
larize the day amongst us. All of us are more careless than once we were in regard to this balustrade;
we permit and do things which once would have
shocked us. It may be true, as things now are, that
more Sunday work is done on the Monday than on
the Sunday paper; but if there were no Sunday paper
the Sunday work on the Monday paper would not be
necessary. But that is not the only point: the reading of the paper on that day secularizes the day. It
considerably defeats the divine thought of the day.
Sabbath-day means rest-day, pause-day, cease-day.
God lifts up his voice and says, Stop! Rest! Business men, you need rest, and you ought to obey
God. Your mind should have a chance to get out
of the ruts. Let the market quotations alone. To-
day dismiss the world. Remember that you belong

to another country, even an heavenly. You are candidates for eternity. A newsman has often told me
that he cannot attend church, because he has to supply so many church-members with Sunday papers.
Instead of being lifted by the day, you drag it down
to your level. Body, mind and soul cry out for the
Sabbath. Workingmen have rights; they are crying for rest. Be not deaf to these manifold voices.
If you must walk on Sunday with your children,
take them into the Sunday-school and come yourself
into the Bible classes. I would have Sunday for you
and your children " the happiest time of all the glad
New Year."

Happy is that land and blessed is that family where
the Sabbath is kept holy, and where God is loved and
served! A week without Sunday is like a country
without the fragrance of flowers or the music of
birds. It is like a year without summer, nothing
but bleak, barren, frozen winter. It is like a night
without a morning, nothing but sorrow, darkness,
death. Sunday is God's benediction on a troubled
world. He speaks his "Peace" and the voice of
trade and strife ceases, and God's hush alone is
heard, while every heart is uplifted in holy song, or
bowed in humble prayer. Such is God's idea of
Sunday: such should be ours. Has this balustrade at
any point been broken? Repair the breach; keep the
balustrade intact. Then shall America ride upon the
2

high places of the earth, for the mouth of the Lord
hath spoken it.

THE BALUSTRADE OF FAMILY PRAYER.

II. On the roof erect also the balustrade of
Family Prayer. God hath set the solitary in families. He has instituted the family relation; and the
relation carries with it the duty of instruction and
worship. This is the oldest institution, and family
worship is of ancient and divine origin. Behold the
family altar builded by Noah! Remember that when
Abraham built a tent for himself he built an altar for
his God. We never read that Lot built an altar;
no wonder that he looks toward Sodom, and then is
soon found in Sodom. When Isaac and his servants
pitch their tent and dig a well, they build their
altar. Listen to the grand resolution of Joshua, "As
for me and my house, we will serve the Lord!" Oh
for more Joshuas and Hannahs as heads of families!
The New Testament and the early history of the
Church contain many similar examples. I cannot in
this connection go at length into the duty and the advantages of family prayer and religion; but many of
these advantages suggest themselves at once to you.
You have observed that family life is often the best
test of genuine piety. Bunyan's Christian makes
Talkative a saint abroad and a devil at home; he
tells us that Talkative's "house is as empty of religion

as the white of an egg is of savor." It is on record that when Mr. Whitefield was asked whether some one was a Christian, his reply was, "How can I tell? I have never lived with him." It is to be feared that in the rush and bustle of our modern life the old-fashioned methods of family instruction and prayer, when all the family and servants were called together, are now much neglected. The Jewish law made the father a prophet and priest in his own family; at the paschal feast he slew the lamb, and he sprinkled the blood on the lintels of the door; he also taught the statutes of the Lord to his children and servants. Philip Henry, in his family circle expounding to them the Word of God, reminds us of one of these grand men of the olden time; it was in this atmosphere that Matthew Henry grew up to be the best expositor of the mind of the Spirit which the Church has yet produced. The notes taken of his father's expositions at family prayers were the foundation of his wonderful "Commentary." Much to be pitied is that home where the voice of prayer is never heard. It is a roof without a balustrade, exposed to danger and death; it is a house without a roof, into which the storms of temptation fall, and on which the sun of trial will beat with scorching ray. John Randolph said that men charged him with being a French infidel; he denied the charge, but confessed that he would have been one if he had not been taught to bow at his mother's knee and say, "Our Father." Every day should begin with prayer. Let us talk to God before we talk much to men; let us begin every duty, and decide every question with prayer. It is said that Pericles, the great Athenian statesman, would not address an audience until he had prayed to the gods, and that Scipio, the Roman general, would not undertake any affair of importance until he had passed some time alone in the temple of Jupiter Capitolinus. The examples of Paul and Christ are still more in point. Remember how earnestly Jesus prayed before entering on his great undertakings! Read the gospels with that thought in mind. Where else do you find such an example of prolonged, fervent and trusting prayer? Remember Paul's requests for prayer; remember also his own references to his habit of prayer. Do you say you have no time? Excuse me, you have. What is time for, but to serve God here and to enjoy him hereafter? David found time amid his manifold cares and great responsibilities to pray three times a day; Daniel found time when he was prime minister in Babylon to pray three times a day; Luther used to say, when his gigantic toils pressed upon him, that he could not get on with less than three hours of prayer; General Havelock rose, it is said, at four, when the hour of marching was six, rather than lose the period of prayer and communion with

God. No time! Do not say that. You know you have.

Do you say you cannot pray? Stop a little; you can. What is prayer? Eloquence is not needed; the publican's prayer sent him down to his house justified. It is the pastor's duty to press home this neglected privilege. I have read that when Richard Baxter went to Kidderminster, there were whole streets in which there were only two or three praying families; and that, when he left, there were whole streets in which there were only two or three families that were not praying families. His influence pervaded the town; he canvassed its houses; family altars were built, and the voice of prayer and praise girdled the town and went up acceptably into the ear of God.

Make the hour of family worship the most joyous of the day. Regard it not so much a duty as a privilege. Husbands and fathers, let nothing rob you of the privilege and glory of being the high-priests in your own families. The children will never forget this hour, even if they are scattered to the ends of the earth. When the great Dr. Nott lay dying they bent over him to catch his whispers, and they heard him murmur, "Now I lay me down to sleep." The only thing we can never forget is what is learned in childhood. When you are building the soul-houses of your children, put around them the

balustrade of prayer. Is there a family represented
here in whose home the family altar has been torn
down? Go home and rebuild it. Is there one in
which it never has been erected? Go home to es-
tablish it, I beseech you. Ask a blessing at your
table; gather your children about you, and around
them and yourselves throw the balustrade of family
prayer. To-day think of these two blessed balustrades—the Holy Sabbath and Family Prayer, and
may God help us to erect and maintain both!

II.

Divine Balustrades.

(PART II.)

" When thou buildest a new house, then thou shalt make a battlement for thy roof, that thou bring not blood upon thine house, if any man fall from thence."—DEUT. xxii. 8.

LAST Sunday while discussing this text attention was called to the two important balustrades— Observance of the Sabbath, and the Practice of Family Prayer. There are still other balustrades to be placed upon the roof of our soul-house and family home. We are exposed to danger from many quarters; we ought to fortify our roof at every point. Our roof is to be a place both of defensive and offensive warfare. The inspired writer tells us to be watchful against our besetting sin; but it is often equally necessary to be on our guard concerning sins that are not besetting, as we suppose. We flatter ourselves that we are safe as to them, and the enemy takes advantage of our indifference to danger and our neglect to provide the munitions for defence.

23

There are, therefore, other balustrades to be erected and to be kept constantly in position.

III. Permit me to mention as one of these—Reverence for the Bible. This is a day of the making and reading of many books. Every age produces its supply. Solomon said three thousand years ago, " Of making many books there is no end;" were he living now he would write that sentence in great capitals. But the majority of books die with the age which gives them birth. Many of these books ought to die; they are bad and that continually. But others are like " the tree of life, which bare twelve manner of fruits and yielded her fruit every month, and the leaves of the tree were for the healing of the nations." A good book is a wonderful product of brain and heart. Milton uttered a great truth when he said: " Books are not absolutely dead things, but do contain a progeny of life in them to be as active as that soul was whose progeny they are; nay, they do preserve as in a vial the purest efficacy and extraction of that living intellect that bred them. A good book is the precious life-blood of a master-spirit, embalmed and treasured up on purpose to a life beyond life." These words are especially applicable to the Bible, which by pre-eminence is called " The Book." No book that has ever been written has exercised so vast an in-

fluence, and has so stimulated to noble achievements
as the Book of God. Some men think it is smart to
speak sneeringly of the Bible. Such men are taking
quite unnecessary pains to advertise their own ignorance. They are usually those who have never read
the Bible, nor, for that matter, much of any other
good literature. They have picked up at second-
hand some objections to the Bible—objections which
were exploded hundreds of years before these men
were born—and parade them as if they had made a
great discovery. Men of learning and thought know
better, even though they may not themselves be
Christians. To the Bible we owe what is noblest in
literature, most enduring in art and sweetest in song.
Not to speak just now of its higher merits, I claim
for it the first place because of its literary worth. As
history the Bible should be studied; it is the oldest
history, and it records the oldest events. It illustrates the best elements of historical writing; and
every page gives proof that its writers wrote in the
conscious presence of the living God. Its biographies
are matchless; this difficult species of writing is here
seen to perfection. Truth dominates every part; in-
firmities and excellences are faithfully portrayed:
this fact is an evidence of its inspiration; uninspired
writers would have denied or concealed the sins,
and would have magnified or created the virtues of
their heroes. Its influence on language is wonder-

ful; it has fixed the form of many languages; and it
ennobles and exalts every language into which it is
translated. Think of its influence on music, painting and sculpture. Without the Bible Milton's poetic
genius had never so loftily soared and sung. He
had to go to the Bible for his high theme, and the
music of "Siloa's brook that flowed fast by the
oracle of God" gives its charm to his lofty verse. The
Bible gave Raphael his inspiration. He ascended
"the holy mount" and gazed on the transfigured
Christ, else the world had never seen his immortal
"Transfiguration." A passage from the Bible gave
Handel his text for a great oratorio as he was about
to leave England for Ireland. On that scripture he
composed his immortal work, known at the first as
the "Sacred Oratorio," and now as the "Messiah."
But for the Bible Spenser's "Faerie Queene," Pope's
"Messiah," Cowper's "Task," Wordsworth's "Ode
on Immortality," and Bryant's "Thanatopsis" had
never been written. Rapt prophets and inspired
apostles gave these writers their themes, thoughts,
and poetic fervor. Let the names of Michael Angelo, Haydn, Beethoven, Mendelssohn, Tasso, and a
score more, suggest further to you how to them all,
and to others working along the different lines of
their own inherent genius, the Bible furnished
themes and inspiration.

Think of its poetry. True, it has no great epic

poems; but it has dramatic elements in several books, although perhaps no great drama. But of didactic poetry it has noble specimens; its pastoral poetry is unsurpassed; and its lyrics, inspired by God, lift the heart up to him. Milton declares that the Greek and Roman classics are unworthy to be compared with Zion's songs. Sir Daniel Sandford, a critic of marked ability, as quoted by William Walters in his "Claims of the Bible," says that, "In lyric flow and fire, in crushing force, in majesty that seems still to echo the awful sounds once heard beneath the thunder-clouds of Mount Sinai, the poetry of the ancient Scriptures is the most superb that ever burned within the breast of man." Carlyle, in speaking of the book of Job, says, that apart from all theories about it, it is one of the grandest things ever written with pen: "Sublime sorrow, sublime reconciliation; oldest choral melody as of the heart of mankind; so soft and great as the summer midnight, as the world with its seas and stars! There is nothing written, I think, in the Bible, or out of it, of equal literary merit." Its influence on legislation is great. Egypt and Phœnicia borrowed from its light; so indirectly did Greece; Rome borrowed from Greece, and the laws of Rome have exercised a great influence on the codes of Europe and America. A distinguished French jurist, himself an atheist, in comparing the laws of Moses with those of other great lawgivers says: "Lycurgus wrote, not for the people, but for an army; it was a barrack he erected, not a commonwealth; and sacrificing everything to the military spirit, he mutilated human nature to crush it into armor. Solon could not resist the effeminate and relaxing influence of Athens. In Moses alone do we find a morality distinct from policy, and for all times and peoples. The trumpet of Sinai still finds an echo in the conscience of mankind— the decalogue still binds us all." Disraeli says in his "Tancred," "The life and prosperity of England are protected by the laws of Sinai. The hard-working people of England are secured a day of rest in every week by the laws of Sinai." Friends, it was a matchless code, and it was given with indescribable majesty.

> "The terrors of that awful day, though past,
> Have on the tide of time some glory cast."

Could we trace the secret sources of the greatness of all the heathen nations, it would be seen that their only valuable lights, in all departments of human genius, were kindled on God's altars: and that their loftiest strains of poetry were but echoes of Hebrew song. Blessed Bible! It is the flower of all the world's books; it is the softest pillow for the aching head; it is the best balm for the broken heart; it brings heaven down to earth; it lifts earth up to heaven. Hear Disraeli again: "In times of sorrow we fly not to Byron, Wordsworth or Shakespeare, but to David. The most popular poet in England is the sweet singer of Israel, and by no other race except his own have his odes been so often sung. It was the sword of the Lord and of Gideon that won for England her boasted liberties; and the Scotch achieved their religious freedom chanting upon their hillsides the same canticles which cheered the hearts of Judah amid their glens."

But let us remember that the Bible is not an amulet, not a charm. It must be read, studied, incorporated into our souls. It is the sword of the Spirit; we must have the keen eye and the supple wrist to use it well. Let us hide the truth in our hearts, that we sin not against God. Let us plant every spot of the soul with the good seed of the kingdom, and there will be no room for the plants of error to grow. Let us fill the heart with the wheat of God's Word, and the world's chaff cannot enter. The best way to preach down error is to preach up truth. So also let us train our children. Never speak slightingly or jokingly of the Bible! Do not talk too much about the original, and about different manuscripts. Let the sweetest memories of childhood gather about the family altar and the old family Bible; and those memories will be balustrades to many a soul struggling with the world's fierce trials. Around your house and heart let this battlement stand. God has

spoken; we have his very words. They are life and
power; they came from God; they lead to God.
Throw around the boys and girls the instructions of
him who spake as never man spake. Then if our
children scramble up and fall—as perhaps they will,
for children have gone from family altar and Bible to
perdition—their blood will be upon their own heads.
God save us and our children! As we fold them to
our hearts, do thou, O God, folds us and them to thy
hearts!

PERSONAL FAITH IN CHRIST.

IV. In the last place, erect this balustrade also,
Faith in Christ as a personal Saviour. This unites
all the others and completes the balustrade about the
house. If we have this faith in our hearts we shall
regard the Sabbath, observe family prayer, and respect the Bible. The three former battlements fit in
and blend with this one. We began with the flower
and fruit of the religious life, and we come back to its
root of personal faith in the Lord Jesus. You know
that, at least in mediæval architecture a battlement
was "a wall, or parapet, on the top of a building, with
embrasures, or open places, originally designed for
military purposes, the lower part offering facility for
the discharge of missile weapons, and the higher serv-
ing as a protection against the enemy; now it is used
in church towers and other buildings as an orna-

ment." Personal religion is both. It protects while it adorns; it adorns while it protects. It arms from head to foot. It overcomes the world; it masters the flesh; it tramples on Satan. Without it no man is safe; with it you are prepared for life's trial, and sure of heaven's victory. Even the old Latin proverb says that "a man without religion is like a horse without a bridle." Do you point me to some noble man without religion? I say, Whatever of nobility he has is due to some elements of religion which he has. Give him more religion, and he will manifest a grander nobility.

Remember that the battlement is to be built when your house is built. A most important law is here suggested—the law of prevention. An ounce of prevention is better than pounds of cure. Better far is it to put a balustrade on the roof than to be picking up maimed and mangled bodies on the pavement below. Formation is better than reformation. A child kept from gross sins and won to the Lord Jesus is a greater miracle of grace than is the man who had fallen low and was then picked up. A child's conversion ought to be a cause of greater joy and gratitude on earth, as it is in heaven, than the conversion of a gray-haired sinner. In the one case a multitude of sins have been prevented, and a life is saved to good and to God; in the other case, it is true that a soul may be saved from hell, but many sins have

been committed, and the life is lost to good and to
God.   In our joy at the conversion of old men, of
drunkards and of other great sinners, we are in danger
of forgetting the value of a child's conversion, and
also of forming a wrong estimate of God's grace in
its accomplishment. · The balustrade should be put
on when the house is built.   " When thou buildest a
new house, then thou shalt make a battlement for
thy roof," is the divine requirement.   You have no
right to expose yourself, your family and friends to
danger, and then, after many have been destroyed,
talk of building the battlement.   This is unpardon-
able folly; this is unspeakable guilt.   Do not trifle
with danger.   Try not how near you can drive to
the edge of the precipice; the good driver sees how
far away he can keep.   Do not take risks.   Do not
tempt the devil.   Young men, don't talk of " sowing
wild oats."   That is the devil's phrase.   That is not
the way to get rid of a bad crop.   Remember that
whatsoever a man soweth, that, precisely that, shall he
reap.   Bear with me, then, while I warn, rebuke, and
encourage you.   Put up the battlement now, because
you are in peril; your life may be lost even if your
soul should at the last be saved, and a lost life is a
fearful loss.   Put up the battlement now, because
you are exposing others to peril; you are the centre
of a circle of influences, and other lives by your conduct may be saved or lost.   Put up the battlement

now, because if not now you may never do it; time
hastens; this year will soon be gone; carry not over
into the new year a burden of unforgiven sin; the
balustrades ought to have been put up long ago;
youth is going, age comes, death approaches. O
men and women! Come to the Lord Jesus this day,
I beseech you; and having so done, "we know that
if" the balustrades of "our earthly house of this tabernacle were dissolved, we have a building of God, an
house not made with hands, eternal in the heavens."

3

Knowing and Trusting God.

"And they that know thy name will put their trust in thee.—Ps. ix. 10.

WE must bear in mind, in order rightly to understand a text like this, that in the Bible the word *name* stands for character, or for the person to whom it is applied. The expression "the name of the God of Jacob" is equivalent to saying the God of Jacob; "for my name's sake" is simply for my own sake. The word name in the text really stands for the word God. To know God's name is to know God—to know his character, to know himself; and the word "know" means to regard with care or with reverence. God is revealed in the Bible by many names, and each name gives us a distinctive element in his character or an important event in the history of his revelation of himself. It thus comes to pass that treasures of truth lie hidden in these distinctive titles; they are revelations of God's glorious attributes. A similar law is illustrated when fresh names

34

are given to men to commemorate their great deeds. It occasionally happens that the original name is forgotten by the great mass of the people, and the man goes into history under the acquired title. British and American history furnish many illustrations of men in civil and military life whose great achievements gave them new names—names which contain much of their history, and which reveal their true character. In like manner God's names are progressive manifestations of his character; they are memorials of the victories of his grace and love.

This is a deeply interesting subject. It will repay us to examine carefully the Bible with this thought in mind, observing the reasons for the new names which God at various stages of his progressive revelation is pleased to give himself. Such names as El and El Shaddai and Elohim, and many other names, illustrate this law.

At this time, however, we shall limit ourselves to a class of Jehovah titles. Jehovah is God's name as expressive of his personal covenant with his redeemed people. It also sets him forth as the eternally existing One. In Exodus iii. 14 this great name is distinctively ascribed to God: "And God said to Moses, I shall be what I shall be; and he said, Thus shalt thou say to the children of Israel, The I-SHALL-BE has sent me to you." Here God's unchangeable character is made known in the name

which implies his eternal self-existence. The same
idea is frequently taught in other passages of the
Old Testament. We shall consider only six of these
Jehovah titles. Attention has been called to the
fact that four of them are historic, recalling
to after ages national and personal deliverances,
and that the other two are prophetic. These
two shine as diamonds in the brightness of Israel's
future; they look forward to the reign and glory of
Messiah. The first four, then, are historic; the re-
maining two are prophetic; and all the six are profoundly instructive to the thoughtful student of the
Bible. Let us take them in their order in the inspired
narrative.

1. We have Jehovah-Jireh—"Jehovah will see,"
or provide (Gen. xxii. 14). This is the symbolical
name given by Abraham to the scene of his offering
of the ram which was supplied by God in the place
of his son. The name, doubtless, has reference to
Abraham's reply to Isaac's question in the eighth
verse: "God will provide himself a lamb." This is
one of the most ancient and most precious titles of
God. We are all familiar with the story of which
it forms a part. The mysterious command of God,
the loyal but sorrowful obedience of Abraham, the
patient submission of Isaac, the journey undertaken,
the third day, the sad preparations, the outstretched
hand, the arresting voice, and the substitute pro-

vided—these are all familiar as parts of this strangely
interesting and divinely appointed narrative. We
are permitted to enlarge upon the lessons here taught.
We may drop the narrative at this point, in order to
receive the precious truths which it suggests.

Jehovah will provide for our temporal necessities.
We may not, indeed, fare sumptuously every day; we
may not wear purple and fine linen—but verily we
shall be fed. If God clothes the grass of the field,
which to-day is and to-morrow is cast into the oven,
shall he not most certainly clothe us, who are made
in his own image? He commands us to pray for
our daily bread, and he assuredly will give that for
which he commands us to pray. His people are assured that they shall not hunger nor thirst; that
though the young lions shall suffer hunger his people shall not want any good thing. He will also
give his people intellectual wisdom: "The secret of
the Lord is with them that fear him." There is
here the statement of a solemn and a universal law:
the attainment of religious knowledge follows the
law of attainment of every other kind of knowledge.
Only those who seek find; only those who submit to
the law reap its fruits. No man is qualified to pronounce on religious truth except he possess religious
knowledge by personal experience. Christ is the
centre of all truth. Toward him all lines of truth
converge; from him they diverge. All truth lays

its crown at his feet. Men who reject him who is ·
the truth cannot truly acquire the truth which he
imparts. Other things being equal, those who bow
lowly at his feet are best fitted to walk on the lofty
heights of truth of every kind. All science should
be studied with this thought. Chemistry, geology,
and astronomy are revelations of thoughts of God.
Every angle and triangle, every sine and co-sine, reveal and emphasize thoughts of the Eternal. Every
flower and plant, every tree and mountain, are the
manifestation and revelation of sublime and divine
thought. Only as nature is studied with reference
to nature's God can nature be fully understood.

But our God is especially Jehovah-Jireh in the
matter of spiritual food. God's people shall not lack
the food their souls require for growth in grace and
holiness. They are a spiritual people; they are born
again of the Spirit; they are made partakers of the
divine nature. This new life must have constant
supplies of spiritual food. In its beginning it desires
the sincere milk of the Word; later it can receive
the strong meat of divine revelation; always it hun-
gers after that bread which came down from heaven.
The soul, no more than the body, can live upon past
supplies. The spiritual nature must have spiritual
food. It is man's highest glory that this earth, with
all its wealth, its honors and charms of every sort,
cannot supply the wants of his immortal nature. If

man were a thing, he might find enjoyment in things; but, being made in God's image, only God can satisfy his desires. He can never find rest until he finds it in the love and on the bosom of his God. God delights in receiving the homage of his creatures, and in supplying their spiritual wants. He will feed his children with marrow and fatness; he will make his grace sufficient for them, and will strengthen them with might in the inner man. The experience of every Christian will justify this affirmation. I appeal to that experience. Has God ever forsaken you? Has not his grace been sufficient for you from day to day? Can you not say to-day, "Hitherto hath the Lord helped me"? Let the past encourage you for the future; let your yesterdays be the prophet for your to-morrows. He that spared not his own Son, but delivered him up for us all, how shall he not with him also freely give us all things? He promises pardon to penitent sinners. He will abundantly pardon to-day. Go to him as did the publican, and like him you shall go down to your house justified.

2. Jehovah - Ropheca — "Jehovah that healeth thee," or Jehovah thy physician (Exodus xv. 26). Let us attend for a little to the connection in which these words stand. The Red Sea has been crossed; the triumphal song of Moses has been sung, and the glorious refrain of Miriam has been chanted. With

some difficulty, perhaps, were the people induced to
leave that shore on which they had witnessed the
defeat of the proud Egyptian and the display of the
power of God. The wilderness lay between them
and Canaan. That wilderness must be trodden
Into it they plunge : but in that wilderness of Shur
they had no water. This was especially trying to
those who had been accustomed to the bountiful and
delicious waters of the Nile. They are in a dry
and thirsty land, where no water is. Three days
pass; they reach Marah; their hopes are high; their
disappointment will be great. Marah is bitter—un-
pleasant to the taste, and injurious to the health.
They cannot drink. God was testing their faith and
loyalty. Moses prayed. In obedience to the command of God he cast into the water the tree which
the Lord had shown him, and of a sudden the waters
were made sweet. God's people then and now must
learn to obey. If obedient, God promises that he
would put none of the diseases and plagues of Egypt
upon them. God is no respecter of persons. It has
been well said that a disobedient Israelite will fare
no better than a rebellious Egyptian. In connection
with this additional promise of warding off disease
he gives us his new and glorious name, Jehovah
Ropheca—"I am the Lord that healeth thee." They
had been preserved from disease and death in Egypt
by their obedience to God; and the same condition

still holds. Jehovah provides the Lamb as the atonement for sin, and he also provides the means of protection from disease. The Psalmist beautifully expresses this truth, and unites these two thoughts,
when he says: "Who forgiveth all thine iniquities;
who healeth all thy diseases." Jesus Christ is the
true Physician. It was foretold of him that he
should bear our sin and our sicknesses. He is the
true Jehovah-Ropheca. Without adopting the extreme view of those who have come to be known as
faith-healers, we must still admit that sin and disease are mysteriously connected. Weakness and sin
came together. To one whom he healed Jesus said:
"Sin no more, lest a worse thing come unto thee."
We are looking forward to the time when there will
be no sickness—when no inhabitant of that blessed
realm shall say, I am sick. Christ is the Healer of
the diseases of the mind as well as those of the body.
The man who wandered among the tombs needed the
healing presence of Jesus Christ. The lunatic child
was cured by the divine Lord. He is also the Physician for the soul. Soul-sickness is the most terrible
of diseases. A sin-sick soul only Christ can heal.
In the thirty-second Psalm we have a description of
such a soul. There was no rest all day long; the
moisture was turned into the drought of summer.
Not until the transgression was forgiven and the sin
covered could there be rest and peace. Only when

the pardoning voice of Christ is heard may sinful man or woman "go into peace." May the healing power and forgiving grace of Christ be felt now, alike in body and soul!

3. Jehovah-Nissi—"Jehovah my banner." Exodus xvii. 15: "And Moses built an altar and called the name of it Jehovah-Nissi." This symbolic title was given by Moses to the altar which he erected on the hill where his hands, uplifted in prayer, had caused Israel to prevail, and had secured the defeat of Amalek by Joshua and his chosen warriors at Rephidim. Perhaps the significance of the name is found in the allusions to a staff which Moses held as if it were a banner during the battle. As it was raised or lowered, the fortune of the battle turned in favor of the Israelites or of the Amalekites. God is thus recognized in this memorial as the deliverer of his people—as he who leads them to victory, as he who is their rallying-point in time of trial and danger. We remember that the Amalekites were the descendants of Esau, and that they hated the Israelites because of the birthright and blessing which were given to Jacob and not to Esau. Their country was south of the Philistines; they therefore went out of their own territory to assail Israel. This is the first case of Gentile antagonism to Israel since they marched out of Egypt. Israel must now gird on the sword and contend with stout arm and brave heart for

national independence. Joshua is here mentioned
for the first time, and comes before us as the com-
mander-in-chief in this expedition. The Amalekites,
prepared for battle, cowardly and basely fall upon
the rear, and slay the faint and feeble of the people.
Moses with his wonder-working rod takes his stand
on the neighboring hill. Joshua fights; Moses
prays; both serve God's Israel and Israel's God. The
rod which had summoned the plagues of Egypt, and
under which Israel went out of the house of bondage,
is still mighty as the symbol of God's presence and
power. That uplifted rod appealed to God, but the
strong arm of Moses became weary; and he sits
while Aaron and Hur alternately stay up his hands
until the going down of the sun. Israel or Amalek
prevailed according as the hands of Moses were up
or down. Amalek is defeated; Israel is triumphant;
and Jehovah gave the victory. Either on the hill
overlooking the battle-field, or on the field itself, the
altar with this inscription was erected. God was
recognized in this memorial altar as the deliverer of
his people.

The battle rages still. The hosts of sin are many
and strong, but God is still Jehovah-Nissi. Too
often we forget God and trust in ourselves or in our
fellow-men. Then defeat is inevitable. How gloriously ring out the words of the Psalmist: "The
Lord is my light and my salvation; whom shall I

fear? the Lord is the strength of my life; of whom
shall I be afraid? When the wicked, even mine
enemies and my foes, came upon me to eat up my
flesh, they stumbled and fell. Though an host
should encamp against me, my heart shall not fear."
The Psalmist also rejoicingly says, " Thou hast given
a banner to them that fear thee, that it may be displayed because of the truth." The Apostle Paul also
affirms that our weapons are not carnal, but spiritual.
Jehovah-Nissi is still our battle-cry.

> 'Mid mightiest foes, most feeble are we,
> Yet trembling, in every conflict they flee ;
> The Lord is our banner; the battle is his,
> The weakest of saints more than conqueror is.

4. Jehovah-Shalom—"Then Gideon built an altar
there unto the Lord, and called it Jehovah-Shalom"
(Judges vi. 24). The altar erected by Gideon in
Ophrah was so called in memory of the salutation
given him by the angel of Jehovah. The meaning
of this title is " Jehovah peace," that is, Jehovah gives
peace, or prosperity. It is equivalent to the salutation, " Peace be unto thee." This altar was the token
by fire of the coming victory over Baal. Peace was
to be the fruit of that victory. The story is deeply
interesting, but there is not time to give it in detail.
We are reminded of the triumphant words of the
apostle in his letter to the Romans: " Therefore, being justified by faith, we have peace with God

through our Lord Jesus Christ." The Jehovah-Shalom of the Old Testament is the "God of peace" of the New Testament. The apostle also assures us that the God of peace will bruise Satan under our feet. It is also affirmed that Jehovah will give strength unto his people, and that Jehovah will bless his people with peace. The angels sang the song of peace on the night of Christ's birth. Before he left his disciples he gave them the legacy of his peace, and as he came back to them triumphant from the grave, his salutation was, "Peace be unto you!" And after his ascent to heaven, the apostle speaks of his Father and ours as the "God of peace." This peace God's people may enjoy. It is a peace which the world can neither give nor take away—a peace which passeth all understanding; a peace which is Christ's peculiar gift, and which is the foretaste of the bliss of heaven.

It has been sweetly enjoyed in hours of sickness and sorrow, and in times of pain and death. When sin is forgiven, and the heart is reconciled to God, peace comes as a heavenly visitant to go no more out for-ever. A ship may be tossed violently upon the sur-face of the deep, but by its side an iceberg will float undisturbed by wind or wave. The secret of its calmness of movement is that the greater part of its bulk has gone down deep into the sea, where the waters are undisturbed by wind or wave. When a believer's life goes down into the deep things of God, he, too, can calmly outride every storm and gloriously triumph over every foe. May the peace of God abide with us evermore!

5. Jehovah-Tsidkenu — "Jehovah our righteousness."

"*In his days Judah shall be saved, and Israel shall dwell safely; and this is his name whereby he shall be called, the Lord our Righteousness.*"—JER. xxiii. 6.

As we have already seen, the four previous Jehovah titles are historic; but this and the one that follows are prophetic. This epithet is applied by the prophet to the Messiah. It is also applied to Jerusalem, because that city was symbolic of the future prosperity of God's chosen people in the Christian dispensation. Many believe that the epithet here given by Jeremiah ought to be regarded as ascribing to the Messiah the name Jehovah; others, that it is simply an expression of the faith of Israel that through the Messiah righteousness shall flourish. One loves to adopt the former rather than the latter interpretation. This title of God has often been the watchword of his dear children. They love to associate it with the apostle when he speaks of "the righteousness of God, which is by faith of Jesus Christ unto all and upon all them that believe." Every thoughtful man recognizes his need of a righteousness which naturally he does not possess. He knows that the law is exceeding broad; and he feels the need of a righteousness equally broad. He knows that God cannot look upon sin with pleasure; and he feels his need of a righteousness on which the eye of the great God may rest with complacency. He feels the need of a righteousness richer than that which angel ever possessed; and he knows that if Christ be his righteousness he shall be clothed with a robe pure as the light and more glorious than angel or seraph ever wore. He rejoices when he realizes that Christ is in him as his hope and glory. He can triumphantly say, with heroic and devout Paul: " There is, therefore, now no condemnation to them which are in Christ Jesus." He can fearlessly ask, with the same matchless apostle: " Who is he that condemneth? It is Christ that died, yea, rather, that is risen again, who is even at the right hand of God, who also maketh intercession for us." Jehovah-Tsidkenu, as we have often sung in McCheyne's familiar hymn, will be our inspiration in life, our watchword in death, and the theme of our loftiest song in eternity.

6. Jehovah-Shammah—"Jehovah there."

" *It was round about eighteen thousand measures: and the name of the city from that day shall be, The Lord is there.*"— EZEK. xlviii. 35.

This title designates the place where God dwells.

It was the symbolic name given by Ezekiel to the spiritual vision of Jerusalem which he enjoyed. It belongs to the class of figures descriptive of the New Jerusalem in the Apocalypse. In the Old Testament it is a prophetic description and type of the Church in the Christian dispensation. It reminds us of the beautiful name Immanuel—"God with us." Perhaps its primary reference was to the situation of Jerusalem after the exile, but in the New Testament the vision is enlarged and carried forward until the symbol is more fittingly applied to the heavenly home of the saints of God. God has promised to dwell with him that is of a contrite and humble spirit; so that of the heart of every lowly believer we may say, Jehovah-Shammah. God has also promised to be in the place of prayer; for did not the Master himself say, "Where two or three are gathered together in my name, there am I in the midst of them"? This is a peculiarly precious promise. From the redeemed heart we go out to a place where redeemed men and women meet, and once more we can say, Jehovah-Shammah. But the circle must still be enlarged. Not only does God dwell in the redeemed heart and in the place of prayer, but also in the redeemed earth: "And I heard a great voice out of heaven saying, Behold, the tabernacle of God is with men, and he will dwell with them, and they shall be his people, and God himself shall be with them, and be their God." Over every home in this redeemed earth may be placed the title Jehovah-Shammah. Glorious title—precious privilege—happy people! There are no people so blessed as the people of God. Heaven comes down to earth and abides in their hearts and homes. Paradise is regained in their sweet experience.

We are carried back to our text: "They that know thy name will put their trust in thee." Will you trust him here and now? They who know him best trust him most. That men do not trust him is the best evidence that they do not know him. If you knew him in all the sweetness and blessedness of his character, you could not but love and trust him. All the revelations of God in his word and works are such as to lead men to trust him with all their hearts. Come to him now, and you shall know him as ever present, Jehovah-Shammah, as your righteousness, Jehovah-Tsidkenu, as your peace, Jehovah-Shalom, as your banner, Jehovah-Nissi, as your physician, Jehovah-Ropheca, as your provider, Jehovah-Jireh, as your all and in all forevermore.

4

IV.

God's Answer by Fire.

1 KINGS xviii. 22–40.

THE topic which comes before us for our consideration to-night is God's answer by fire on Mount Carmel. The portion of Scripture which contains the history I have already read to you, as found in the first Book of Kings, the eighteenth chapter, beginning with the twenty-second and going to the end of the fortieth verse.

Having considered last Sunday evening the convocation on Mount Carmel, and having heard Elijah's personal question to the assembled people—"How long halt ye between two opinions?"—we are now prepared to consider this great and memorable scene. This part of Elijah's history is in perfect harmony with the entire purpose of his earthly mission. He came to restore God's broken covenant, and to lead God's Israel back again to God's worship. Just at this point in their history some great and decisive act was necessary in order strikingly to arrest the attention of the nation, and in order most sublimely to give God an opportunity to declare his presence and his power. This was, then, the appropriate time for a great display of power and authority on the part of God. Ahab and the court on the one hand, and Israel as a whole on the other, had been bowed down because of the long and terrible famine. They are now more ready to listen to God's voice and to understand the manifestations of his will.

It was a time of judgment for all classes; it was a time of terrible defeat for the foes of God; it was a time of glorious victory for the friends of God. The question is now to be decided, once for all, whether Jehovah is God or whether Baal is God. The day, therefore, marks an epoch in the history of Elijah, in the history of Israel, and in the history of God's redemptive plan. This day marks the climax of Elijah's life; it is the very acme of his earthly career and divine mission. His personality always shines out with great grandeur, but never was it so grand as on this occasion. His heroism was always lofty; but to-night we shall see him sublimely heroic as he stands for truth and for God, alone among the hundreds of Baal's worshippers. I make bold to say that there is no picture in all secular history, and that there are but few pictures in sacred story, that can for grandeur and sublimity be compared with this picture. Here, as nowhere else in the Bible, we see the greatness and glory of a man who stands for God in the presence of God's bitter foes. No wonder that poetry with lofty genius, no wonder that painting with the brush of inspiration, no wonder that music with consecrated art should find in this grand theme the occasion for noble achievement! The great composer has poured his soul into his immortal oratorio; and nowhere is it grander than when he represents the wild cries of the priests of Baal and the humble, trustful supplication of the prophet of God. I am glad that in the course of these Sunday night sermons we have now reached the point where we may sit for a time in God's house, and have this sublime picture on Mount Carmel pass in panoramic vision before us.

No doubt Ahab and the people of Israel expected that now the heavens would be opened and the earth be refreshed with rain; but Elijah's God knows that a work of preparation is necessary before he can unlock the windows of heaven. There must be evidence of genuine repentance and sincere reformation. To grant the blessing of rain before the people had given evidence that they had turned from idolatry to the worship of the true God would be no kindness. Elijah, therefore, proposes to put the whole question now to a decisive test—whether Jehovah is God or whether Baal is God. Doubtless all through this transaction he acted under divine instruction; otherwise his conduct would not be justifiable. He would have been guilty of presumption had not God so led him; but God had doubtless so communicated his will that this test should be made, and that this result should be secured. It was great condescension on the part of God that he should go into competition with Baal—into competition with an idol which, as Paul tells us, "is nothing in the world." But God knows that his claims are incontestably right, and he is not afraid to submit them to the severest test on the part of man. We know that God's truth to-day will stand the fire heated "one seven times more than it was wont to be heated," and it shall come out without the smell of fire upon one of its pages. I am willing to submit Christianity to all forms of honest criticism; for I know that its pure gold will shine in its heavenly glory and matchless splendor all the brighter because of the test to which it has been thus subjected.

But Elijah stands before us very conspicuously as the leading actor in this strange drama. We gaze at him for a moment as he stands there alone; and his solitary condition would excite our sympathy did we not know that he is not alone, for he who is "mightier than the mightiest" is by his side. He is like a sheep in the midst of wolves; he is like a lily in the midst of briars; he is like a solitary oak on the mountain-top, while God's thunders roll, God's

lightnings flash, and God's tempests sweep the
mountain's brow. But, as the oak is only the more
firmly rooted when so exposed, so Elijah's faith
grasped the eternal God; and there he stood. We
glance at him a moment, with his sheep-skin cape,
with his long, flowing, shaggy locks, with his humble but dignified mien, as he walks out in the path
which God has thus appointed for him, as we listen
to his proposal. I need not stop to read it to you;
you are familiar with it. You may ask why he did
not propose that God's answer should come by water
and not by fire? There were special reasons why it
should be by fire on this occasion. Fire, in connection with sacrifice, is the symbol of atonement; and
the truth taught by an atoning sacrifice must be emphasized before the sin of the people could be taken
away. Should God send the fire, this would show that
the sacrifice was well-pleasing. God was accustomed
to answer by fire. This fact was perhaps another
reason why this form of test was suggested. Go
back to the very dawn of history, and you discover
that God answered by fire in the case of Abel's sacrifice. God manifested himself by fire in the destruction of Sodom and Gomorrah; he manifested
himself by fire when Moses stood by the burning
bush; by fire when Israel stood by the base of trem-
bling Sinai, while God's law was proclaimed to the
assembled hosts. God answered by fire when the

sons of Aaron, Nadab and Abihu, offered strange
fire upon God's altar. And in the memory of some
living in Elijah's time God had gloriously answered
by fire at the conclusion of Solomon's dedicatory
prayer, when fire came down from heaven, and the
glory of God filled the Temple so that the priests were
not able to continue their worship. And gloriously
God answered by fire on the day of Pentecost, when
the Holy Spirit came as a tongue of flame and "sat
upon each of them." A further reason, no doubt,
was because Baal was regarded as the god of fire,
the god of the sun, the god of heaven. He was the
"heaven-sun-fire" god. This was, therefore, a conspicuously just proposal on the part of Elijah; for
fire was Baal's own element. If the test had been
by water it might have seemed that Elijah was taking an unjust advantage; but Baal was the god of
fire, and if he could not succeed when he was operat-
ing in his own realm, then he was worthless indeed.
We see Elijah's justness, and at the same time his
skilfulness, in making this form of test. It shall be
a trial by fire. "And all the people answered and
said, It is well spoken."

You discover further that Elijah gives the prophets
of Baal the precedency. They are many. I imagine that at this point the priests of Baal would gladly
have evaded the test; but it was not possible for them
so to do. They rely, perhaps, on the doubt as to

whether Elijah can accomplish his purpose. They
rely, perhaps, also, on the hope that by some deceit-
ful movement, some sleight-of-hand practice, they
may conceal fire among the wood. We know that
it was not considered beneath the dignity of these
idolatrous priests, by subterranean channels and various other forms of deceptions, to inject fire into the
wood, and thus lead the worshippers to suppose that
fire had come from their deity. This Elijah seems
to have anticipated; so he takes pains to assert that
they "shall put no fire under," and is watchful and
alert throughout the whole proceeding. They took
the bullock, dressed it, and began to call on Baal. It
is morning. I suppose that many of them spent the
previous night on the mountain. Look—the sun is
rising! Baal is the god of the sun. They wait until
they see its first rays before they begin their petition;
and as they see the eastern sky beautiful with the
crimson and gold of approaching day they begin
their prayer. They cry out: "Ha Baal anaenu! Ha
Baal anaenu!"—"O Baal, hear us! O Baal, hear
us!" Mountain height echoes to mountain height
with their wild cries. All through that forenoon
they cry unto Baal. And now it is noon. Elijah
has spent all these morning hours in perfect silence.
The sun is now pouring down his scorching rays
upon the mountain-top. Surely, at this hour, if ever,
the fire shall come! But no! the heavens are silent,

the altar is cold. Now Elijah speaks his cutting
words—words of biting sarcasm; words of sharpest
irony; words that must have lashed these priests into
perfect fury. Some have been surprised that Elijah
should so speak. As Dean Stanley says, his words
seem to lack "the general humanity of the New
Testament and the general seriousness of the Old."
But Elijah was not frivolous. On the contrary, he
was never more intensely in earnest than now. To
scorn such folly as that of which they were guilty is
the right kind of treatment. He answered fools according to their folly. Sometimes, as has been suggested, the only answer to make to certain self-con-
ceited opponents of religion is fie, fie! pooh, pooh!—
just as you would talk to children; because reason
will not have weight with such unreasonable opponents of truth and God. I do not know where in all
literature you will find words of more biting sarcasm;
and they nobly served their purpose. Elijah was
princely. It is glorious to look at him and inspiring to hear him. Alone on the mountain-top he
walks among those excited priests like a king; he
speaks as if he were master of the situation, as indeed he was. Some of his words contain a most
suggestive euphemism, which reduces Baal to the
lowest degree of contempt. Elijah was conscious
of God's protection, else he would not have dared
to utter words of such terrible severity. He throws

such contempt on their miserable god that argument
is unnecessary.

It is certain that they took Elijah at his word.
They cried the more to the silent heavens; but the
silence was not broken, the heavens heard not. The
altar was cold; the fire fell not at that noonday hour.
And now they begin, according to their custom, to
cut themselves with knives and lancets until the
blood gushed out and mingled with the sacrifice.
The dervishes at the present day cry out in their wild
worship, Allah! Allah! They whirl about with great
speed; they leap and dance to the sound of cymbals
and drums; they even cut themselves with knives
and swords, until they faint from pain and loss of
blood. Baal's priests were driven to like frenzy. In
their fury they leaped from the altar, while their
blood streamed over their torn vestments and lacerated bodies. But the heavens were mute; the altar
was cold. No god, no man, regarded their cry.
"There was neither voice, nor any to answer, nor
any that regarded."

And now it is afternoon—about three o'clock. It
is about the very time when, years after, the great
Sacrifice was offered—not on Mount Carmel, but on
Mount Calvary. Elijah comes forward. He is calm
and majestic. There is authority in his words;
there is dignity in his acts. "Come near unto me!"
"And all the people came near unto him." The

ruined altar with his own hands he rebuilds, with twelve stones. He comes not to introduce a new religion, but to re-establish the old. The twelve stones preach a sermon regarding God's covenant and the twelve tribes of undivided Israel. The separation of the ten was not recognized by God. Round the altar a trench is dug; the wood is put in order; the bullock is cut in pieces and laid on the wood. From the neighboring well, as there is reason to believe, four barrels of water are taken and poured upon the sacrifice and the wood, that there might be no possibility of imposture. Three times over this is done, until the water ran round about the altar and also filled the trench. All is now in readiness. Will the fire come? Will God hear? This is the time of the evening sacrifice, the holiest hour in Israelitish worship. It is drawing toward sunset, and yonder in the Temple at Jerusalem the priests are offering their evening sacrifice as the sun sinks behind Olivet. Elijah is preparing to plead with God. Gaze on the picture! See him as he retires a pace or two! Follow him for a little as he makes his preparations! All is now ready. This is a sublime sight. Every eye is upon him. Bravo man! God help him! For if he fails, his own body, before the sun shall set, will be cut into pieces, and will be lying beside the body of the bullock on the altar. If he fails, God is dishonored and Baal triumphant. He is calm and dignified; his trust is in the Lord his God. He offers his prayer. It is simple and sublime. Look at it! You discover as you examine it that it is very short. There are no vain repetitions. He is trustful as he lifts his heart toward God. "Lord God of Abraham, Isaac, and of Israel, let it be known this day that thou art God in Israel, and that I am thy servant, and that I have done all these things at thy word! Hear me, O Lord, hear me! that this people may know that thou art the Lord God, and that thou hast turned their heart back again."

You will discover, as you listen to the prayer, the title which he here gives God. He is the "Lord God of Abraham, Isaac, and Israel." Just as Elijah had twelve stones in his altar, indicating that the twelve tribes were not separate in God's purpose and covenant, so in this prayer he recognizes the covenant relation between God and his people. You discover that he uses two pleas: first, God's glory, and second, the people's good. He has ceased speaking. An unearthly stillness is over the mountain. The priests are breathless. The assembled hosts watch and wait with wildly throbbing hearts. Shall God hear? O God, hear Elijah's prayer! Hush! look! the fire is coming! It falls; it strikes the altar! In a moment more the sacrifice is consumed, the wood is burned, the stones are consumed, and the dust; and the fiery tongues lick up the water that was in the trench.

God has answered by fire! Elijah is victorious; Baal is overthrown. Glory be to God for his wondrous mercy to Elijah his servant!

The effect upon the people is marvellous. They fall upon their faces for a little; and then they wake the echoes amid the mountain peaks with the war-cry, "Eli-jah-hu, Eli-jah-hu! Jehovah, he is the God! Jehovah, he is the God!" In a moment more the priests of Baal are seized, as guilty offenders against God's law, according as it is recorded in Deut. xiii. 5-11. At the command of Elijah, Ahab not opposing, they are dragged down the mountain-side. The people are aroused; Elijah's word is law; the old zeal for God is rekindled; the people recognize that these priests have been deceivers, that they have opposed God and the highest interests of the whole kingdom. They are accordingly brought down to the banks of the Kishon. Executioners are numerous. The priests are slain, and are thrown into the dry bed of the Kishon. When the storm comes, as it will in a little time, the Kishon shall be filled with a rushing torrent, and these crimsoned waters shall bear these dishonored bodies into the depths of the blue Mediterranean.

I cannot stop to speak at length of the charge of cruelty which has been made against Elijah. We are to remember that we are in the Old Testament, not in the New. Bear in mind, also, that these men

forfeited their lives because they violated the law.
They were guilty not only of sin against God, but of
crime against the nation. God was the head of the
State and the Church: and Elijah was his vicegerent.
Not as a barbarous conqueror, but as the appointed
executioner, did he inflict deserved punishment on
these great sinners When God accomplishes great
national reforms he often sacrifices many lives.
When God delivered England from some of her
fiercest foes he made Cromwell his Elijah. When
God destroyed slavery in America he sacrificed a
million of Americans; and men said, "It is terrible;
but a million lives for the freedom of four million
slaves are well spent." That was God's providence.
This is God's providence. There is no great difference between God's relation to the destruction of the
four hundred and fifty priests of Baal (for the four
hundred priests which fed at Jezebel's table seem to
have declined the test by fire), and his relation to
the destruction of a million of men in our war. It is
God working through different instrumentalities. If
men would only reason they would see this truth.
They are unreasonable in thinking that God was
cruel in Elijah's case, while they see no divine cruelty
in the arbitrament of civil war, or in the destruction
of life in great epidemics caused by sinful neglect of
sanitary and moral laws.

And now, follow me in a suggestion or two. The

first one is this: Men and women, you must decide
who will be your God. You must decide, I tell you;
you are on trial to-night. Who is your God? Is it
gold or worldly ambition? Is it self or Christ? Who
is your God? You are on trial to-night. As God's
messenger I urge you to decide this question. "If the
Lord be God, follow him—if Baal, then follow him."
Yes, follow him if he is God. Who is your God to-
night, man and woman? Have you recognized God
to-day? Have words of prayer been spoken by your
lips? Have your knees bowed at any altar? I give
these priests credit for their earnestness. See how
they cry, from sunrise till noon! See how their blood
is mingled with their sacrifice! They rebuke us. Ah!
will you give the answer to me to-night, "Jehovah
is my God, Jesus Christ is my God; I have enthroned
him in my heart?" Can you say it?

The second lesson is this: The time is coming
when the men who worship the world and self and
sin shall cry, and there shall be no answer—no one
to regard their prayer. In the Book of Revelation
we have a wonderful description of a prayer-meeting
—a great, a solemn prayer-meeting. "The great
men, the rich men, and the chief captains, and the
mighty men, and every bondman, and every freeman" made up this great meeting. They hid themselves in the dens and in the rocks of the mountains,
and they said to the mountains and rocks, "Fall on

us and hide us from the face of Him that sitteth on the throne, and from the wrath of the Lamb!" But the rocks do not fall; the mountains still stand; the prayer is unanswered. Oh, if you worship any god other than God you shall cry in vain! The hour of sickness, distress, and disease and death shall come; and you shall go into the dark valley of the shadow of death with no staff to support you. Oh, how terrible to live without God and to die without hope! —to go out into blackness and darkness alone—no friendly eye to see your steps, and no loving ear to hear your cry! That is terrible!

You will notice, third, that God has done more to convince us than he did to convince Israel on Mount Carmel. There has been a greater fire kindled than that on Mount Carmel. That was great; it was, indeed, supernatural. It burned up the pieces of the bullock first, then the wood and stones and the dust. The usual course which fire takes was reversed. That was a wonderful occasion; but a more wonderful thing has occurred. The Son of God has come. The Word was made flesh. He has sanctified the cradle, for he was a babe; he has sanctified motherhood, for he was born of a woman; he has blessed childhood, for he was a child. God came from heaven in the person of his Son, and tabernacled in human flesh. The cradle is more wonderful than Elijah's altar, the carpenter shop in Nazareth than

Elijah's altar. Blessed be God, Mount Calvary is
to Mount Carmel as substance is to shadow! And yet
you are unmoved; you have not cried unto Jesus as
your Prophet, Priest, and King. I tell you, in sober
truth, it will be worse for you in the day of judgment
than for the priests of Baal, if you refuse Jesus Christ
as your Saviour.

And, lastly, God still answers by fire. The fire of
his Holy Spirit is his witness. He answered by
fire on the day of Pentecost. He still answers by
fire—the fire of love, the fire of Christian devotion
in the hearts of his saints. And he will answer
scorners by fire. The Bible speaks of those who are
" reserved unto fire." Christ is yet to come in " flam-
ing fire," taking vengeance on them who know not
God. The Apostle tells us " Our God is a consuming
fire." Oh, may God answer to-night by the fire of
his Holy Spirit in the hearts of us all, for his
name's sake!

5

V.

Obedience the Test of Love.

"If ye love me keep my commandments."—JOHN xiv. 15.

THIS verse is the beginning of one of the most remarkable sections of this chapter. It is introduced here with a certain degree of abruptness. As you know, many times during this discourse Christ spoke words whose design was to comfort his disciples. Now, however, he promised, as we shall soon see, to send the Spirit, part of whose office was to be the Comforter of his people; but Christ teaches that in order to enjoy the comfort of the promised Spirit they must render strict obedience to the divine requirements. We have before us, then, in this verse this morning, the practical test of love—obedience. The whole round of Christian duty is here summed up in this one word—obedience. As love is the fulfilling of the law, so that fulfilment in harmony with

66

the principle of love is manifested by practical obedience to the divine requirements.

Obedience Gives Comfort.

You will observe that in comforting the disciples Christ teaches them to keep his commandments. We may not expect a blessing from God except we render obedience to God. The way of duty is evermore the way of peace and joy. If we do the duty of to-day God will give us the blessing of to-day; but if we fail in our performance God necessarily fails in his fulfilment. You notice that this practical test of love lies in this chapter between two gracious promises—that contained in the fourteenth verse, " If ye shall ask anything in my name, I will do it," and that contained in the sixteenth verse, " And I will pray the Father, and he shall give you another Comforter, that he may abide with you forever." Almost all commentators have been struck by the abruptness with which the text is introduced; but some have not been ready to see its connection with what precedes and with what follows. If the remarks I have now made are correct you will not fail to see the connection. This command, then, lies between two promises; and, in order that we may receive either promise, we must obey the command. God cannot give us the blessing except we obey the command. If we are to ask in the name of the as-

cended Lord for blessings in prayer we must render
loving and obedient service. After Christ had shown
his love to his disciples he appealed to their love to
him. John gives us in his first epistle, fifth chapter and third verse, an evidence of our conversion,
when he says: "For this is the love of God, that we
keep his commandments." Paul speaks in Romans,
thirteenth chapter and tenth verse, the same language, when he says: "Love is the fulfilling of the
law." Love prompts to every duty; love inspires to
every sacrifice; love gives wings to our feet as we
run in the way of God's commandments; love cushions the yoke of duty so that it becomes easy; and
love lifts the burden of service so that it becomes
light. Evermore, enjoyment of God is the closest
neighbor to obedience to God.

Obedience the Best Proof of Love.

It is observable, also, that Christ here teaches the
disciples that the best way to show their love to him
is by obedience. They were overcome with grief at
the thought of his departure; and he teaches them
that actively obeying is a more genuine manifestation
of love than pouring out useless tears at his departure. "Obedience is better than sacrifice" is an Old
Testament proverb, which is abundantly illustrated in
the New Testament. Indeed, obedience is the very
highest form of sacrifice—for it shows that we make

a sacrifice of self and of selfish interests. Not sentimental sighing and crying is the true way to illustrate genuine love on the part of the disciples toward
their Lord. Love can never be satisfied with mere
sentiment; love is never inoperative. Love marches
out along the line of practical service; it rejoices in
the slightest command of Christ. Love obeys. If
the commandment be deemed small, the love that
keeps it is thereby the greater love. It never asks,
Is this command essential to salvation? Love knows
that the keeping of all Christ's commands is essential to obedience. We may, indeed, do what Christ
commands us and yet not keep his commandments.
No man keeps his command if he does so with any
other motive than that of loyalty to Christ. Motives
of self-interest, worldly advancement, or spiritual
prominence utterly rob even a good act of its true
spirit. You may thus obey the command, and yet
not in the full sense keep the command. In order to
keep it, it must be kept purely and solely because it
is Christ's command. That is the Christian's highest authority; that is his last and highest form of
service. Christ has said it—that is enough. A
Christian inspired by love never asks, " How little
can I do and win heaven?" He simply asks, as did
Paul when stricken down on the Damascus highway : " Lord, what wilt thou have me to do?" No
Christian man ever occupies a more unenviable po-

sition than the man who stands beside a cross and
asks, "Is the taking up of that cross necessary to my
salvation?" He ought to blush to ask such a question. He ought simply to listen to his Lord's voice,
which says: "Take up thy cross and follow me."
Let him step out and take it up. Observe the min-
uteness of Christ's language. He says: "Take up
thy cross." Too many of us drag it. It is heavy
when we drag it; but, taken up, it will soon take us
up; the cross that we hold will soon hold us. Does
Christ command me to believe in him? Then I
will do it. Does Christ command me to be baptized?
Then I will do it, because Christ has said it. He is
the highest authority.

Obedience Brings Blessings.

You observe also that when Christ would tell his
disciples how to receive conditional blessings he
commands them to obey him. He had given great
and precious promises; but their fulfilment depended
on certain conditions. Our obedience is necessary to
God's bestowment. Rewards from God to disobedient children would be putting a premium on disobedience. That God will never do. He loves you too
much to give you the richest blessings of his grace
while you refuse to render him the obedience of your
heart. Men often want all the blessings of a Christian life before they are willing to take the first step

in the Christian life. They linger at the wicket-
gate, unwilling to step through until God gives them
all the experiences of a long Christian life. God can
never give them the Christian's joy until they perform the Christian's duty. The blessings of that
pathway are experienced only in that pathway.
Standing outside the gate you cannot have the blessing of those inside the gate and running in the path
of duty. I am sometimes amazed, as I speak with
inquirers, that they do not discover this truth. They
want all the peace which the Christian enjoys before
they are willing to give Christ their trust. Christ
commands them to come unto him and he will give
them rest; but they want his peace before they will
give him their trust. You must take Christ at his
word. You must obey; you must go in the way of
duty; and in the very act of obedience Christ will
meet you and flood your soul with joy. On the morning of the resurrection, when the women came to the
tomb, they saw not Jesus; but they saw an angel,
who said: "Go quickly and tell his disciples
that he is risen from the dead." They were disap-
pointed; they saw not his body—but still they obeyed
the command of the angel. We are told that they
"did run to bring his disciples word." We read
next: "That as they went to tell his disciples, behold
Jesus met them." How blessed! They were running from his tomb—the very spot where they ex-

pected they should see him, at least in death; and
now, as they are running in the path of obedience,
Jesus meets them by the way, and his "All hail!"
filled their souls with joy.   Precisely so does Jesus
meet with us.   When the ten lepers went, in obedience to Christ's command, to show themselves to the
priests, the healing power came upon them.   You
must obey Christ; you must give him your trust;
you must believe in him.   Believe him in the dark.
Anybody can believe in the light.   Take him at
his word; and, my word for it, his word for it, the
darkness shall be scattered and the glorious light
shall shine upon your souls.

God must obey his own law in the bestowment of
blessings.   He is not harsh, not arbitrary, not fickle,
not capricious in dealing with men.   The spirit of
obedience on our part is necessary, that we may receive the highest form of spiritual good.   This is
the divine law.   Christ cannot be a Prophet to any
man to whom he is not a King—not a Priest to any
man to whom he is not a King.   He is a Prophet to
instruct only when he is a King to command.   He
is a Priest to atone only when he is a King to command.   If I refuse his kingship I refuse also his
priesthood and his prophethood.   Only as I bow at
his feet and accept his kingly authority can I receive his prophetic instruction and his priestly ab-
solution.   Here is the divine Trinity of offices in

which Christ appears Prophet, Priest, and King.
Rejecting him in the latter office, I cannot receive
him in either of the former. Now, I hold that this
is sound common sense. There is nothing, in one
way, mysterious in religion. The supernatural, in
a very real sense, is the natural. This principle of
God's government in religious matters holds in all
God's relations with men in every sphere of life. It
must, I am sure, commend itself to every thoughtful
hearer in this audience. It is in harmony with a
universal law. To enjoy health you must obey the
laws of health. God bestows health along the line
of recognized law; and if you will run against that
law God cannot give you the blessing which its observance insures. The same is true in matters of
intellectual attainment. You must follow the laws
of intellectual growth, you must submit to these inevitable conditions, if you are to receive the blessings
of intellectual possessions. There can be no divorce
between the condition and the blessing. In order to
make progress in music, or painting, or any art, you
must submit to the principles that underlie that art.
Obedience is necessary to attainment. This we all
understand. The soldier must obey, else he ceases to
be a soldier. It will not do for him to set up his
own authority. He must march in obedience to the
word of the commander. This is the essential condition of discipline in an army and of success in war.

Precisely so is it in religion. Nothing is love to God
which does not shape itself into practical obedience.
It is simply useless for you to indulge in the thought
of love to God if you do not obey God. It is said
that after a great battle the officers met in their tent
and discussed the question as to who was the bravest
soldier of the day. One said, "It was he who made
a tremendous onset," another, "He who came into
hand-to-hand conflict with the enemy and overcame."
"No," said the commander; "the bravest soldier
was he who had lifted his arm to strike, and when
the sound of retreat was heard his arm paused in
mid-air and he struck no blow. He was the bravest
soldier to-day."

Obedience Gives a Foretaste of Heaven.

Love to God, then, is necessary to the highest enjoyment, both here and hereafter. It gives a foretaste of heaven here and now. You have heaven
in your souls as you sit in these pews, just in proportion as you have the love of God in your souls.
That love makes heaven hereafter absolutely certain.
There can be no heaven anywhere to the man who
does not love God; there can be no hell anywhere to
the man who does love God. That man has heaven
in his soul wherever he goes, whatever he does. If
it were possible for a Christian man to be in perdition, it would cease to be the place of torment; it

would immediately become for him a place of unspeakable bliss and glory. There was a time in my
life when I sometimes thought God was arbitrary;
possibly I thought him harsh in some of his dealings
with men. A better understanding of those dealings
convinced me, and must convince you, that God never
condemned any man to everlasting punishment.
Nowhere in the Book of God, nowhere in the records
of eternity, nowhere in the providence of God has
he ever condemned a man to hell. Men go themselves; they go downward rather than upward.
They stumble over God's word; they despise God's
invitations; they stumble over Christ's cross; they
turn a deaf ear to Christ's prayer. I say it rever-
ently—God cannot stop them except he destroy the
laws of freedom with which he has endowed them.
If you charge God with your fate you show that you
deserve your fate a thousand times over; you show
that you are false to your own conscience and to
God's revelation. Since your infancy God has been
wooing you to his arms and heart. You have
turned a deaf ear; you have despised the pleadings
of his love.

If all the wretched inhabitants of hell were to be
admitted to heaven it would be no heaven to them
while they continued to hate God. That hatred
makes hell. There can be no heaven anywhere to a
man who hates God. To shut up in the regions of

despair men who hate God is a greater kindness to
them than to admit them into his immediate presence. Were you to go to these wretched saloons,
and to take all the people you can find there and
bring them into the house of God, they would be
perfectly wretched. They would say, "Let us out!
We want the ribald song, the blasphemous oath, the
intoxicating cup." Some of you have a foretaste of
heaven in the place of prayer, but to those it would
be a foretaste of hell. Put them into heaven, and
they would be unspeakably miserable. What they
need is not a change in external condition, but in
heart, in life, in purpose, in all their relations to
God. So I say, without fear of contradiction, that
if a man loves God he has heaven everywhere. If a
man hates him he can have heaven nowhere.

OBEDIENCE CLEARLY PROVES LOVE.

But a man asks, "Can I know whether or not I love
God?" Most assuredly you can know. We have
the practical test which is the topic of my remarks
this morning. It is the test of obedience. Do you
obey God? If you constantly obey God, no matter
how you feel for the moment, you love him. Right
feeling will come with obedience. Men act quite
too much by impulse. I wish sometimes that the
word "feeling" were blotted out of our religious
vocabulary. A man says he doesn't go to prayer-

meeting, "because he doesn't feel like it." What has feeling to do with duty? We are saved by faith, not by feeling. Many a time a man goes into his office when he doesn't feel like doing his work. You can work yourself into right feeling. Often the literary man sits down when he has none of that ecstasy and bliss which come when mind and soul are filled with lofty thought. How often did Dickens sit down, seize his pen simply from a sense of duty, and drive it in cold blood for a time! But soon the right feeling came, and soon joyous emotions would throb for utterance. Soon the words would run from his pen-point, until page after page would testify to the work of the morning. These principles apply with literal truth in the Christian life. Do your duty. Why should a man not bow to Jesus Christ? Why should you not say, while I am speaking, "I know that I am a sinner, but I will trust Jesus Christ here and now"?

Couldn't you say that, man? Will you thus determine, woman, in the pew at this moment: "Here, O Christ, just as I am, I give myself to Thee"? Then say, "I have done it; I will never take it back; I will go out into yonder street Christ's man, Christ's woman; I will do my duty, and con- fess him before the whole world." So obeying Christ, be assured that peace and all right feeling will come into your soul; and you shall know by a blessed experience that you are truly Christ's child.

I am glad of this practical test which I have given you this morning. I wanted to talk to you in a plain way. I know many often ask the question, "Do I love the Lord or not?" I know it often gives them anxious thought. Obedience to his commands answers the question. Our own wills must be turned into sympathy with Christ's; running in parallel lines with Christ's there will be no cross. This submission is the significance of baptism: *buried* with Christ. The old man as dead is to be buried; the new man rises to walk in a new life. Blessed symbol! Glorious obedience! Divine Redeemer, help us to show that we love thee by keeping all thy commandments!

VI.

The Bible and the Higher Criticism.

THE apostle here exhorts us to submit all forms of faith to their appropriate test. The word which is translated prove is a very strong expression; it literally means to test by the art of the assayer; it is the word which would be applied to the testing of metals or similar substances. The apostle warns the Thessalonians against receiving statements regarding religious truth on mere assertion. They are exhorted to apply fitting tests, and then to reject what is false and to adopt what is true. The same exhortation is appropriate still. God makes a direct appeal to our reason in regard to the subjects of our faith. Reason and revelation, when both are properly understood, are not contradictory. God through the prophet Isaiah distinctly says: "Come now, and let us reason together." The decisions of synods and councils are not necessarily authoritative.

79

Christianity always and everywhere is the friend
of free and fair inquiry. But we must remember
that it is quite as important to hold fast good things
as it is to prove all things.

The Church of Christ is to expect criticism. She
must not shrink from it; indeed, she cannot help
challenging it. She is a city set on a hill. The
Church does not fear criticism; she fears nothing
but error and sin. Truth seeks the light, comes to
the light, rejoices in the light. Error loves darkness, grows in darkness, and reluctantly comes into
the light, which at once reveals and rebukes its de-
formity. A true Christianity knows that correct
knowledge, and not gross ignorance, is the mother
of genuine devotion. A true Christianity welcomes
truth from whatever quarter it comes and by whatever messenger it is brought. A true Christianity
cares more for truth than for the opinions of the
greatest of men; she says evermore, as Jesus said
to those who asked, " Master, where dwellest thou?"
and as Philip said to Nathanael, who thought no
good thing could come out of Nazareth, " Come and
see." She submits all her premises, processes, and
conclusions to the full sunlight of the most critical
examination. She has absolutely nothing to conceal.
In the encaustic tiling at the entrance to his home,
Lord Tennyson, we are told, has the words, " Truth
against the world." A true Christianity will write

·these words at the head of every sermon, on the first
page of every book, and on the heart of every disciple. In this spirit the Church ought to go forth to
meet her critics. Criticism is the act or art of judg-
ing; the judgment is not necessarily unfavorable,
but even when unfavorable the Church, as the child
and champion of truth, will go forward fearlessly
and even joyfully to meet it.

Our knowledge of the Bible is necessarily progressive. It is evermore true that there is more light to
spring forth from the Word of God. The Bible as
a revelation of an infinite God must evermore be
beyond the full comprehension of finite men. We
can apprehend its truths; we cannot comprehend
them in all their significance. Each generation may
be expected to make advances in the apprehension
of the Bible over the preceding generation. What
science has absolutely proved is a truth of God in its
sphere as really as what revelation has affirmed.
God is one; truth is one. God cannot contradict
himself. What he has taught in Genesis must
harmonize with what he has taught in geology,
when both are rightly interpreted. Between a true
science and a divine revelation there must be entire
harmony. Our contention is only against a science
falsely so called. Science and philosophy are necessary factors in all religious thought. Theologians
who speak derogatively of the influences of philoso-

6

phy really only oppose one system of philosophy
against another. This scientific spirit is in the atmosphere to-day, and can neither be denied nor despised. A true theologian will not attempt to do the
one nor the other. As well might he resist the law
of gravitation, or the movings of the tide. But our
holy religion is never the enemy of truth wherever
found. A true science is the handmaid of Christianity; it is the minister of truth and God. We
need have no fear of the "higher criticism," as it has
been called. Whatever discovers and declares truth
is of God, and is to be welcomed by his Church.
We are only concerned to know that this or any
other form of criticism does really discover and declare the truth. That is the whole matter regarding
which we should be concerned. We welcome all
forms of right examination. The Bible asks no
favors and fears no appropriate tests. Reason and
conscience have their sphere of authority; but revelation is higher than either or both. Where Scripture plainly speaks, human reason must bow in
submission. God as the revealer and the supreme
source of authority is back of the revelation which
is the channel of that authority.

THE CHARACTER OF THE EXAMINATION.

The Bible should be studied on scientific principles. These principles now dominate in other

departments of inquiry, and have their sphere also
as applied to the Bible. All investigation of the
Bible should bear in mind what is its supreme object
and design. Many critics greatly err at this point;
they forget the real object of divine revelation. The
Bible is not intended to be a treatise on philosophy,
science, or history; it is not a text-book on astronomy, geology, chemistry, botany, or geography; it
is not an encyclopædia or universal dictionary. It
does allude to these subjects, and that with an accu-
racy, eloquence, and beauty that are simply surpris-
ing. Its avoidance of the dangers into which heathen cosmologies have fallen is inexplicable if we
deny its divine inspiration; the cosmogony of Moses
receives the confirmation of the science of our
own century. It has been well said that, "there
is in the book of Psalms alone more loving descriptions of nature than in all Greek and Roman
literature;" and yet such descriptions and allusions are merely incidental. Some of these, however, anticipate many of the discoveries of science.
The great design of the Bible is to teach religious
truth; it is to supply man's religious necessities.
This design is ever paramount. Baronius long ago
said: "The Scriptures were given to teach men
how to rise to heaven, not how the heavens were
made." Forgetting these simple facts, ignorant
scientists and equally ignorant ecclesiastics have

waged a foolish warfare. As a result astronomy, geology, and many other sciences have had to fight their way against the opposition of priests, cardinals, and popes. Thank God! a brighter day has dawned. We are learning that all lovers of truth are in many senses pupils in the one school—the school of Christ, which is the noblest university. The Bible is designed to reveal God and man in their mutual relations; it declares man's religious necessities and reveals the divine provision for those necessities. It makes allusion to nations only as they stood related to the development of this spiritual purpose. It thus comes to pass that what Voltaire called an "insignificant Syrian tribe" fills so large a space on the inspired page; that Egypt is scarcely mentioned between the time of Moses and Solomon; that Assyria, after a single passage in the Book of Genesis, is passed over in silence for fifteen hundred years!

Many criticise the Bible because it is not, and never proposed to be, what they have imagined it ought to be. It is not a universal encyclopædia, although it is wonderfully encyclopædic; not a universal history, although it is the oldest and noblest history. Within its own sphere it is authoritative and infallible. To insist upon its historical and scientific inerrancy is to mistake its true design and controlling purpose. We do not admit its errancy as many have affirmed it; but neither ought we to

allow ourselves to believe that if errancy, historical
or scientific, can be proved, the Bible is therefore
errant and unauthoritative on religious subjects.
Those who say that if an error is found in the date
of some ancient king or kingdom, or in the number
engaged or killed in some ancient battle, therefore
we must give up the inspiration of the Bible and
the divinity of the Lord, are guilty of illogical reasoning and of a foolish surrender to the foes of revelation. They ought not to stake the defence of the
citadel on maintaining an unimportant outpost.
Inharmony in the details of testimony in our courts
is not construed by judges and juries as necessarily a
contradiction of the main fact, if on that point the
witnesses harmonize. I have heard officers who
were in the battle of Gettysburg contradict one another regarding some of the details of that historic
conflict; but this discrepancy regarding unimportant
facts would surely not justify a man in affirming
that there never was a battle of Gettysburg. The
Bible is absolutely authoritative on matters of our
spiritual life and faith. This is its chosen sphere;
this is its divine design. We do not admit that
important errors have yet been proved either of an
historical or scientific kind. On this point, "a bill of
particulars" is properly demanded of those who make
the affirmation. They wisely refrain from meeting
this demand; their modesty at this point is surpris-

ingly in contrast with their omniscience at many other points. We simply affirm that all allusions in the Bible to matters of that kind are merely incidental, and do not touch nor affect the main purpose of the revelation.

The critic of the Bible should be sympathetic. This demand is scientific. No man can appreciate the hills except he have mountains in his brain; no man can enjoy the sea except he have oceans in his soul · no man can judge music except his training and nature be musical. The mathematician who asked, after reading Milton's "Paradise Lost," "What does that prove?" was an utterly incompetent judge of that immortal epic. Sir Isaac Newton was right when he said to Dr. Halley, "When you speak about astronomy or mathematics, I am glad to hear you, for you have studied and you understand these subjects; but you should not talk of Christianity, for you have not studied it." Dr. Halley was a competent witness on science, but utterly incompetent on matters of religion. To demand that critics of the Bible shall be sympathetic is to demand only that which we require in critics of science, philosophy, or æsthetics. The cold-hearted, unsympathetic, irreligious critic of the Bible is a monstrosity. He is no more fitted to judge of its truths than a deaf man is to pronounce on music, or a blind man on the merits of a painting.

We have a right also to demand that all investigations of the Bible shall be practical—shall be affirmative or constructive, and not merely negative or destructive. The Higher Criticism might fairly be called general criticism. It discusses not merely the text, but its general relations; its relations to the chapter in which it is found, to the book of which it is a part, to the times to which it is referred, and to its entire environment. "It is," as Professor Stevens, of Rochester, has recently said, "history engaged in verifying the facts of the past." Mere textual criticism is lower criticism; but the investigation which takes up a book, its history, its structure, its credentials, this is called the Higher Criticism. When this kind of examination is applied to the Bible, it is properly called "Biblical Criticism." Let no one fear such criticism, when conducted in the spirit which we have already approved. Let no one denounce men inspired by this spirit and working for the discovery of truth; let no one depreciate the results secured, nor unfairly oppose the methods employed. If the investigation be in a humble and candid spirit, it will but reflect an additional honor on God and his word. It will, without doubt, when so conducted, give fairer conceptions alike of the Bible and its divine Author. If it shall destroy some of the unsightly scaffolds which traditional interpretations and which some human creeds and confessions have erected about the majestic temple of truth, marring its symmetry and robbing it of its divine glory, we shall have cause to rejoice. The Word of our God shall stand forever: that is as certain as that God lives and reigns.

MOSES AND HIS CRITICS.

Many men have entered the arena to tilt against Moses and the Pentateuch. Pharaoh strove against Moses, and he sank like lead into the Red Sea. Jannes and Jambres, the Egyptian magicians, "withstood Moses," and they are named only to show their defeat and humiliation. It has been well said that the Bible is like a cube; when it is overturned, as its foes have thought, it is as high as before. The great scholars of the early centuries attempted to overthrow Christianity and the Bible; but the names of most of them are now utterly forgotten, except as they stand in some way related to the Bible which they vainly attempted to overthrow. Lucian, Celsus, Porphyry, and Julian the Apostate were the leaders of the opposition to Christ and his Church in their respective generations. Porphyry was, without doubt, one of the most brilliant opponents which Christianity has ever had. He was a peerless heathen polemic. He moved boldly into the arena; he was resolved to dethrone Jesus Christ. He anticipated many of the critical methods which are common in our day; but these men would be utterly forgotten were it not that they linked their names, even in opposition, with that Name which is above every name. Jesus Christ is King. From his watch-tower in the heavens he rules this world. His pierced hand is on the helm of the universe. Men have, in their own opinion, been constantly engaged in overthrowing the Bible; but the work has to be constantly repeated. Never did any other book have such vitality. It constantly confronts its foes with new elements of power. It never was mightier than it is to-day. It has overthrown many forms of heathenism, and is now moving forward with head elate and step triumphant to the conquest of the world.

The critics have long been giving their opinion on Moses. It would be interesting to have the opinion of Moses on some of his critics. Those who confronted Moses alive, whether in the court of Pharaoh, on the field of battle, or in the councils of nations, found him a foeman worthy of their steel. Were he not dead his critics would be likely to speak more modestly of their own attainments, and more wisely of his achievements.

Mere destructive criticism is worthy of but little respect. In no other sphere can the minimum of talent so certainly secure the maximum of notice. A child or an idiot with a knife or a hammer, let

loose in a gallery of paintings or a hall of statuary,
can destroy more in an hour than Angelo or Raphael
could create in a lifetime. Destructive criticism
requires but little ability and has but little utility.
At times it may have a mission. It may awaken
curiosity; it may evoke inquiry. Many a minister
can attract no attention by earnestly expounding the
Gospel; but the same man by attacking the Gospel
and denouncing recognized beliefs will have a brief
notoriety in the secular and religious press. By once
hurling a hymn-book from his pulpit at the windows
of his church, a pastor will attract more notice than
by ordinary preaching for a score of years. But
mere destruction is unworthy the ambition of a noble
man and the attainments of a broad scholar. God
often overrules destructive work, however, for the
establishment of his truth. The opposition of Porphyry in his day called into the arena many de-
fenders of Christ and his Gospel. The attacks upon
Christianity in our day have only served to show
the solidity of its deep foundations. Let no believer
be alarmed; let no one feel obliged to steady the ark
of God; God will care for his Word and his work.
The business of the pulpit is to preach the truth and
not to apologize for God and the Bible. A pastor is
engaged in a sorry labor when he is simply unset-
tling the beliefs of men, and robbing the Bible of its
authority and beauty. A man of this character

may have some sphere of usefulness, but it is certainly not in the pulpit or church of God.

What Has this Criticism Done?

It is fair to ask what the Higher Criticism has accomplished. This question we have a right to ask. Once more the Bible is on trial. Many of those who sought its life, as we have already said, are dead, as were those who sought the life of the Child Jesus; but other opponents have arisen in their place. What really has the Higher Criticism accomplished? It has shown, we will admit, that Moses did not write all the Pentateuch. But who, of any intelligence, ever believed that he did? Certainly no reasonable student could suppose that he wrote the account of his own death. The Higher Criticism has shown, we will admit, that in the writing of the Pentateuch various documents were employed. But the critics contradict themselves constantly as to the points of union and cleavage in these documents. One might, before passing judgment on their work, wait until they had gotten through with destroying one another; for the higher critics of one generation spend much of their time in denouncing their brethren of a preceding generation. All the rest of us might be contented to wait until they are through with one another, and then we might gather up the fragments of critics and criticisms which may remain; but we need not take refuge behind these warring critics. Surely no intelligent reader, even though he were not a higher critic, doubts or doubted that various documents entered into the preparation of the Pentateuch. Surely we may give Moses credit for being a man of common sense; his wonderful achievements entitle him, even in the judgment of his harshest critics, to at least this much praise. Even an average historian would take advantage of documents and annals to which he had access in preparing his history. Hume, Macaulay, Motley, Bancroft did likewise; so also do the historians of our day. We could name a widely known American ecclesiastical historian who not only has the assistance of other writings, but, it is said, of many writers in preparing his volumes on the history of the Church. They are not less his because of this method of preparation. Representative higher critics admit that the Pentateuch is written under the guidance and influence of Moses. More we do not need; more we neither claim nor desire. It is, in a special and beautiful sense, a glorious and divine mosaic. What if the accounts given of creation are but a series of grand panoramic views? They may be none the less true. We know that the language is not scientific but scenic; that it is not philosophic but optic, as Dr. Boardman has suggested. Is it not, therefore, the more natural and accurate? We have no difficulty with the conception that in these glowing chapters we have unrolled before us. as before Moses, successive events in great spiritual visions. We did not need the wisdom of the latter-day higher critics to teach us these acknowledged truths. They have told us that Isaiah did not write all the book which bears his name—that there were at least two Isaiahs. Perhaps they are right; perhaps they are not. Internal evidence is not conclusive. We cannot decide such questions in the case of Junius and others of a comparatively recent date. The matter is not important. Personally, I should be glad to know that there were twenty-two Isaiahs instead of two. He is exactly the kind of man whom we should like to see greatly multiplied. Recent criticism may yet shed some light on the interpretation of the Song of Solomon and on predictive prophecy; but as yet it has given us an uncertain twilight.

Has this criticism deepened the piety of the Church? Has it quickened its zeal? Has it led to a greater consecration to work and a stronger desire to live for the glory of Christ and the salvation of men? No positive answer can yet be given to these questions; but this criticism has done good just so far as it has discovered truth; but not when it has simply dealt in mere destructive criticism, and has forgotten that divine charity, which " vaunteth not

itself," and " is not puffed up." The true position for
the Church to take is that of appreciation of truth
wherever found, and by whatsoever messenger
brought: that of patient waiting until undigested
theories are verified and vain speculations are con-
clusively proved. It is needless to oppose unverified
theories; and it is wicked to cling to old prejudices
when new truths are proved. What we want is
neither the old theology, nor the new in itself, but
the true theology. God will not leave us in doubt.
His word is not a system of cunningly devised fables.
It is my firm conviction that the Higher Criticism
has not thus far achieved practical results sufficient
to justify its exaggerated claims; neither has it so
opposed truths previously held as to justify the opposition of some conservative and orthodox theologians.
It is itself on trial. Let us calmly wait; let us be
open, frank, and fair; let us not denounce the motives of earnest scholars who, with us, are seeking
after truth.

There are great basal truths which must forever
abide. Human sin and sorrow are terrific facts.
The birth, life, death, and resurrection of Jesus
Christ are eternal verities. There is a science of
salvation. God's sovereign and eternal love, God's
gracious Fatherhood and forgiving mercy are eternal
verities. Christ lives, and he himself said, in his
matchless intercessory prayer, "This is life eternal,

that they might know thee the only true God, and
Jesus Christ, whom thou hast sent." With un-
daunted heart we stand beside the Cross to-day. In
this sign we shall conquer the world; that Cross is
still the power and the wisdom of God; it is still the
mightiest magnet to draw men from self and sin to
holiness and heaven. We want the old Gospel, old
as eternity and new as the last rays which flooded
the earth with the light and glory of heaven.
Nothing but the bread of heaven can feed the
hungry soul; nothing but the blessed balm of
Gilead can heal the heart's sorrow. Blessed be
God, his Gospel will never lose its power until
Satan is crushed beneath our feet and Christ is worshipped as Lord over all, blessed forever.

VII.

The "With Christs."

THE relation between Christ and his people is most intimate and tender. The resources of language are exhausted in the attempt to describe and emphasize it. Figure after figure, drawn from every department of nature and experience, is used to set forth this relation. Our Lord said: "Because I live, ye shall live also;" thus he shows the nearness and vitality of the union between him and his people. He also calls himself the vine, and describes them as the branches in illustration of the same thought. He also says: "If a man love me he will keep my words; and my Father will love him, and we will come unto him and make our abode with him." This is wonderful language. Observe the divine plural. The thought of this relationship fills us with awe; it sets forth the marvellous condescension of God, and it ought to move every heart with deepest gratitude and holiest love. Our Lord also says: "I in them, and thou in me, that they may be made perfect in one." The apostle Paul expresses the same thought when he says: "For if we be dead with him, we shall also live with him; if we suffer, we shall also reign with him." Kinship with Christ in sufferings implies partnership with him in triumphs. Just before leaving the disciples he said: "Where I am there ye may be also," and afterward at the right hand of God his feelings and purposes are still the same, for from that exalted height he said: "To him that overcometh will I grant to sit with me in my throne, even as I also overcame, and am set down with my Father in his throne."

My purpose this morning is to describe and illustrate some of these relationships as they are presented to us in the epistles. I shall present, in a logical rather than in an historical order, the passages in which the expression "with Christ" is found; but passages containing other expressions, although relating to Christ, are omitted.

1. "*Crucified with Christ.*"—GAL. ii. 20.

Scripture teaches us in many places that Christ literally died for us on the cross. The apostle Paul in the previous verse tells us that he himself was dead to the law, but alive to God. In the verse before us he explains what he means by that statement. We know that only the two robbers were literally crucified with Christ; but the apostle Paul was crucified with him in the sense of dying with him to

7

sin and its sway. His old nature was crucified; he became dead to the world, to the law, and to sin; he was as dead to the ambitions, pomps and charms of the world as if he had been actually crucified. His life was identified with that of his Lord, so that he could properly speak of himself as crucified with him. The death of Christ on the cross for him made him dead to worldly things and evil passions. His highest glory now was to be in all things like his Master. He longed to be bound to him in the closest fellowship. He was willing to share in all respects the shame and ignominy of his Lord's crucifixion. It was his ambition to have fellowship with Christ in his sufferings, and to be made conformable unto his death. He elsewhere expresses a strong desire to know Christ and the power of his resurrection, as well as the fellowship of his sufferings; but although thus dead to sin, he teaches us in the passage before us that Christ lived in him and that he himself lived by the faith of the Son of God. The true Christian's death to sin is often a real crucifixion; it is lingering, painful and ignominious. But he will not come down from his cross until he can say to every sinful tendency, "It is finished." The true Christian is a wonderful paradox. He is dead, and yet he is alive; he lives in the flesh, and yet he lives by faith; he lives a self-life, and yet his is a true Christ-life. Out of the dead enemy to Christ has come the living, lov-

ing, laboring servant of Christ. This is a blessed
crucifixion; this is an honored fellowship; this is a
glorious exaltation. God grant that we may all be
crucified with Christ, and that we may live in, for
and with Christ.

2. *"Dead with Christ."*—ROMANS vi. 8.

If we are crucified with Christ we become dead
with Christ, as is affirmed in the passage now before
us. As Christ was dead in the grave, so we are to
be dead to self and sin. This thought carries us
back to the third and fourth verses of this same
chapter in Romans. There we learn that we are
baptized into the likeness of Christ's death. The
apostle's words are: "We are buried with him by
baptism into death." For a time Christ lay in the
tomb hidden from sight; then he rose triumphant
from the grave. So the believer, in token of his
death to sin, is hidden for a time in the watery
grave; then he rises to walk with Christ in newness of
life. Having been thus dead and buried with him
the apostle says: "We believe that we shall also live
with him"—live with him here and now, and live
with him forever hereafter. The primary reference
is probably to the present rather than to the future
life. As Christ was raised from death, so we were
raised from the death of sin to a life of holy service;
we are dead men restored to life, we are even now

both dead and alive. Baptism thus becomes profoundly significant; it is eminently beautiful and instructive in its symbolism. How glorious would be
the Christian faith if all its professors were thus
dead to sin and alive to God! How truly blessed the
baptized would be! Let us strive to make this our
happy experience. When that experience is attained
our spiritual death and resurrection will be the
promise and prophecy of that literal death in the Lord
which the voice from heaven has pronounced to be
blessed. The Lord, who sanctified the waters of
baptism, has also glorified the tomb of the dead, robbing it of its gloom and lighting it with a heavenly
radiance.

3. "*Hath quickened us together with Christ.*"—EPH ii. 5.

We who were dead are quickened, are made alive
again. We are saved from the death of sin and we
have received the life of Christ. The relation between Christ and his people is such that his resurrection from the grave included our resurrection to
spiritual life. As death locks up the senses and seals
the powers, grace unlocks and opens them to the
light and life of truth and Christ. This is the
Lord's doing, and it is marvellous in our eyes. It is
he that hath quickened us, he that hath raised us up
together, he that hath made us to sit together in
heavenly places in Christ Jesus. It is by grace that

we are saved. Our salvation is possible because
God is rich in mercy and hath loved us with an everlasting love. His love was manifested toward us
even while we were sinners. All our spiritual blessings flow from our union with Christ. If a man be
not quickened together with Christ he is still dead in
trespasses and sins; he is a child of wrath even as
others. These are very solemn words. Their teaching ought not to be misunderstood by us. Have you
felt the pulsation of this new life throbbing in your
souls? If not, you are still among the dead. Awake,
thou that sleepest; and arise from the dead, and Christ
shall give you light. Become to-day, I beseech you,
children of God and joint heirs with Jesus Christ,
and then shall you be inheritors of eternal life.

4. *" Risen with Christ."*—Col. iii. 1.

In the second chapter and 20th verse of this epistle
we are taught that we are dead with Christ, but
when, as we have already seen, we become quickened
together with Christ, we must leave the tomb. The
grave is not the place for living men. When life
once more comes into the soul, the dark and noisome
grave is to be abandoned. We are raised from the
grave of sin to live a life of holiness. He now lives
in heaven, so we in him should now live for heaven;
as he is at the right hand of God, the union between
him and his people is such that their affections must

be set on him and on heavenly things; not on the
things of this earth, its houses and lands, its honors
and pleasures, its ambitions and achievements, but
on heaven and heavenly things.   Nothing short of
heavenly things can be worthy of the supreme affection of an immortal and redeemed soul.   The Christian who finds his highest joy on earth debases his
heavenly birth, dishonors his high calling, and im-
perils his divine destiny.   The child of earth may
mind the things of earth; but the child of glory will
be engrossed with the things of heaven.   He is,
while upon the earth, an eagle encaged; his home is
in the skies.   At times he longs to plume his wings
for a lofty flight.   His treasure, like his crown, is in
heaven where God is; it is laid up with Christ.
These are precious truths.   What manner of persons
ought we to be in all holy conversation and godliness.   All our joys and sorrows, all our trials and
triumphs are but fitting us for the enjoyment of our
glorious inheritance with Christ.

5. "*Hid with Christ in God.*"—Col. iii. 3.

The Christian life abounds in apparent contradic-
tions and in startling paradoxes.   We are poor, yet
making many rich; we are sorrowing, yet always
rejoicing; we are daily dying, yet still live.   The
apostle Paul affirms that he lives, and immediately
adds, "Yet not I, but Christ liveth in me."   So here

THE "WITH CHRISTS." 103

he says to the Colossians, "Ye are dead," and then adds, "Your life is hid with Christ in God." Of course, he uses these familiar words in varying senses. The death mentioned is that of the lower and earthly nature; the life is that of the higher, nobler and diviner nature. All life is born of death. An American poet has sung:

"Life evermore is fed by death,
    In earth and sea and sky;
And, that a rose may breathe its breath,
    Something must die."

Our true life, like a treasure of greatest value, is hidden; it is safely deposited with Christ in heaven where God our Father is. It is too valuable to be entrusted to our keeping; a jewel of such inestimable worth might be taken from us if committed to our care. There is wonderful sweetness in the thought of life thus hidden with Christ. There is here a nestling, trusting and blessed tenderness; there is here a sublime security; there is here a divine inspiration. Blessed, thrice blessed, is that man who can say that his life is "hid with Christ in God."

6. *"Joint heirs with Christ."*—ROMANS, viii. 17.

Earlier in this chapter our attention is directed to the glorious doctrine of adoption. We show that we are truly adopted of God, when we are led by the Spirit of God. When so led we are not simply followers, disciples, or friends; but we are the children of God. The spirit of bondage is utterly gone; we are no longer slaves, but sons. As children rejoicing in our relationship with God, we cry, Abba, Father. We are then heirs of God to an inheritance which he will confer on his children both here and hereafter; but we are more than "heirs of God," we are "joint heirs with Christ." Christ is pre-eminently the Son of God; and all true Christians are so united to him that they become partakers in his glories and sharers in his possessions. He is God's Son by nature; they are God's sons by adoption, but in both cases the idea of sonship inheres. We are the members; he is the head. Every crown placed on his brow surrounds our heads with reflected splendor. Surely no Christian ought to forget his heavenly birth and his glorious destiny. We ought to live above the world. Our heads should be among the stars. This world ought to lose its hold upon those who are so honored of God and so dowered with heavenly glory.

7. *Christians are "to be with Christ."*—PHIL. i. 23.

The apostle Paul appears before us here as a greatly perplexed man. He is in a strait, but it is a blessed strait. We read of David being in a strait between three sad possibilities—sword, famine, and pestilence; but, as it has been well said,

we find Paul here in a strait between two blessings—living with Christ on earth, or being with
Christ in glory. Dr. Adam Clarke and other commentators have called attention to the fact that the
metaphor here employed is suggested by a ship lying
at anchor. The commander of the vessel is in a
foreign port. He feels a strong desire to set sail, as
the word here used implies, and get to his own
country and family; but this desire is offset by the
conviction that the general interest of the voyage
may be best subserved by a longer stay in the port
where his vessel now rides. He is not in a dock, he
is not aground, but rides at anchor, and may at any
hour be gone. Strong winds are already blowing
upon his vessel, which, were it free, would soon drive
it out to sea. Such was the condition of the apostle.
Strong cables of love bound his heart to the Philippians, and yet heavenly influences were moving him
as a gale blows upon a vessel. He was not at home,
but in a foreign land on his Master's business. He
wishes to return; he rides at anchor. He is only
awaiting further orders; but in any case he will do
his full duty. Sick and sorrowful, weary of the
world and its sin, he had a desire to slip the cable, or
draw in the anchor, and sail away to his heavenly
home; but he would not allow misanthropy or personal comfort to prevent him from doing his duty to .
God and to man. He was willing to bear physical

pain, if he could thus serve the church and honor his
Lord. In his thought death was not a sleep, not a
period of unconsciousness. To depart was to be at
once with Christ, and to be with Christ was heaven.
The difference between a Christian and a man of the
world is this love for and desire to be with Christ.
Mere willingness to die is no evidence that one is a
Christian. Pure selfishness may sometimes lead
men to wish to throw off all earthly care and sorrow;
but a true believer looks upon heaven as giving the
opportunity to be with Christ as he cannot be upon
the earth. To the apostle Paul this fellowship was
far better than any earthly friendship. O noble
apostle! O blessed strait! May the spirit of the
matchless Paul in his complete submission to the will
of God, whether for life and service here, or for rest
and glory hereafter, be the dominant spirit in our
lives!

8. "*Reigned with Christ.*"—REV. xx. 4.

We began with the cross and the grave, we have
now reached the crown and the throne. There is not
time to enter now into the full discussion which the
present passage might justify. Perhaps the reference is to the martyred and glorified dead. Certainly
a millennial age of great power and glory is here
. suggested. The controlling influences of the world
are under the direction of Christ and his Church. All

the forces of government and all the influences of social life are in harmony with the Spirit and Church
of the Lord. This condition is the opposite of that
which now exists; now the foes of Christ are often
in the seats of power; now right is often on the cross
and wrong on the throne; but the earth shall yet be
"filled with the knowledge of God;" truth shall
yet triumph and righteousness and peace prevail;
our present hopes shall then be a glorious reality and
our present faith blessed sight. The promise of
Christ will then be fulfilled; those who have shared
his cross shall then be with him on the throne.
Elsewhere in this book our blessed Lord distinctly
promises that those who should overcome should sit
down with him on his throne. Christ's throne is
large enough for all his people. He carries us at
the last in the "overcomeths" of Revelation to his
temple and to his throne. We are, as God's true
children, candidates for crowns and thrones. Our
Lord had prayed, "Father, I will that they also,
whom thou hast given me, be with me where I am."
Before such a promise and prayer reason staggers
and imagination reels. This highest place is within
the reach of the lowest child of Adam. Farther we
cannot go; more than this even God can neither say
nor do. In this promise the Eternal exhausts himself. The thought of this glory is overwhelming.
To lie at Jesus' feet would be heaven; to see "the

King in his beauty," even at a great distance, would
be heaven.   But to sit on his throne—it is too much;
we have no thought to conceive, far less language to
express this indescribable honor.   Christ so loves us
that he longs for us to be by his side; he longs to
show us his glory.   Soldiers of the cross, the victory
shall be yours.   Is the conflict severe?   Are the enemies numerous and strong?   Fear not, ye men of God,
ye followers of the Lamb; ye shall overcome every
foe, through the blood of the Lamb.   On the brow of
the redeemed shall be placed the triple crown—the
crown of righteousness, the crown of life, and the
crown of glory.   Who would not be a Christian?   O
men and women, submit now to the authority of
Jesus Christ.   Listen to the invitations of his love.
See him as on the cross he dies for you.   Be crucified with him on that cross, be dead and buried with
him in yonder grave; be quickened together with
Christ; be risen with Christ.   Let your life be hid
with Christ in God; become joint heirs with Christ,
and then you shall sit with him on his throne and
reign with him for ever and ever.

VIII.

Doing All to the Glory of God.

*" Whether therefore ye eat or drink, or whatsoever ye do,
do all to the glory of God."*—I COR. x. 31.

THE Bible is an intensely practical book. It belongs to all centuries and climes, to all forms of civilization and culture. It is a book of great principles rather than of specific rules. Our relations with men and things change with every hour; it is, therefore, simply impossible for the Bible to give us rules sufficiently numerous and specific to guide our conduct by minute directions amid these changing relations. Human law-makers, in their efforts to circumvent the inventive versatility of law-breakers, have so multiplied laws upon our statute-books that the laws touching some phases of crime are involved in almost inextricable confusion. On the basis of the teachings of the great Mahomet a code of laws numbering seventy-five thousand was compiled; and yet cases soon arose among the followers of the prophet which did not come within the application of the letter of any one of these laws.

The Bible gives broad and fundamental principles.

We have the help of the Spirit of all truth to enable us rightly to understand and properly to apply these principles; so that no seeker after truth need fall into error as to any practical duty. These grand principles are far-reaching and heart-searching. They furnish us with the spirit rather than the letter of rules for moral conduct. The inculcation of a right spirit is better than the enactment of a right law. For the letter may be obeyed while the spirit of the law is evaded. We are commanded to love God with all our heart and our neighbor as ourselves; we are to follow the Golden Rule given by him who spake as never man spake. The spirit of these great principles penetrates every possible relation in life; it meets the master and his servant, the mistress and her maid; it enters the counting-house and the workshop; it confronts the lawyer and his client, the physician and his patient, the pastor and his people. Christ's Gospel stands far above the systems of morality devised by human wisdom. Heathen moralists gave precepts numerous and intricate; but Christ gave a few great principles of universal application.

The text is one of these great laws. It is exceeding broad; it'sends its influence into every relation of life. In the chapter from which it is taken the apostle Paul gives some rules relative to the eating of meats offered to idols; and then sums up his instructions in the all-comprehensive law of which the text is the formulation. By the glory of God we are to understand the honor which is paid him by his creatures; to glorify him, therefore, is to seek his honor in all the actions of our lives. The phrase has many applications in Scripture; but the fundamental idea is the giving of God honor, whether in praise, in prayer, or in a life of honesty, obedience, and purity. We are to glorify him in all the relations of life.

God is to be glorified in our strictly religious duties. This seems to be almost an unnecessary statement. Religious duties, we may say, are for the express purpose of honoring God. All must admit, however, that there is much of self and sin often entering into our holiest duties. The thought is humiliating in the extreme that men instead of preaching Christ crucified may preach themselves glorified; that instead of pouring out their hearts in penitent prayer, they lift them up, Pharisee-like, in thanks to God for their many virtues. Religious work in its loftiest aspects is constantly in danger of being regarded as a trade, of being considered as a means of securing a comfortable living. Religion never made a hypocrite; the want of it makes many. Men never counterfeit what is worthless; when they counterfeit religion they commend it, although they condemn themselves for their want of it. In proportion as churches become financially and socially potent factors in life, is the temptation to engage in religious duties from bad motives strong. Motives must be carefully watched. Benevolent contributions may be for our own glory rather than for God's. Our charity may cover a multitude of sins in another sense than that in which the apostle uses the phrase. Self must be crucified that God may be glorified. Our labor must not be for our own church or our own denomination as its inspiring motive; these have their place, but Christ must have the first place. Self must be dethroned; Christ must be enthroned. No idol must usurp his place; to him our supreme love must be given. God forbid that in our religious work we should glory save in the cross of our Lord Jesus Christ!

GLORIFYING GOD IN BUSINESS RELATIONS.

We are to glorify God in all our business relations. There is danger that we shall make an unwarrantable distinction between our business engagements and our religious obligations. They do not belong to different spheres of duty. We too often act as if Sundays and churches belong to God, and week-days and business houses belong to the world, the flesh, and the

devil. There is a sense in which the house which
has been consecrated to God is peculiarly sacred; but
there is also a sense in which every office and store
may be consecrated to God. Religion is not for Sundays and churches alone; religion is for week-days
and business houses as well. Religion sanctifies
and glorifies every relation in life. If you cannot
take your religion into your business, you must have
a very bad business or a very poor religion. We all
recognize the importance of what is known as "a
call to the ministry;" the man who refuses to heed
this call does so at his peril. But it must not be forgotten that every man is called to some form of ministry in the kingdom of our Lord.

The whole duty of every one everywhere is to glorify God; the exalted privilege of every man is to enjoy God forever. No man is excused from this great
obligation because he refuses to confess Christ; this
refusal but adds to his guilt. If you are engaged in
an honest business for which you have qualifications
and which you are conducting in a religious spirit,
you may rest assured that God has called you into
that business. By giving you ability to perform
your work God has set you apart to that duty; other
business men may not have formally laid their hands
upon your head giving you ordination to that service, but tacitly they have given their approval, and
God has given his blessing. This conception of our

8

daily calling exalts and glorifies it; it makes the lowliest duty radiant with the glory of the loftiest motive. This conception of life and duty converts every office and store, every workshop and factory, every parlor and kitchen into a sanctuary. It makes every counter and desk, every anvil and bench a pulpit from which men and women may preach the Gospel of Christ and in which they are to glorify God. We are to find our opportunity to serve God, not apart from, but in our daily vocation. Any other thought of secular service degrades it and dishonors God.

The apostle Paul often emphasizes this thought. We must emphasize it to-day; we must repeat his words, "Servants, be obedient to them that are your masters, . . . as unto Christ; not with eye-service as men pleasers; but as the servants of Christ, doing the will of God from the heart;" and "Whatsoever ye do in word or in deed, do all in the name of the Lord Jesus. . . ." The needle of Dorcas served God as truly as does the pen of the recording angel. With thread in the garments of the poor it wrought an inscription more durable than if on brass or marble. Her eulogy will be read when the victories of Roman arms and the glory of Grecian arts are forgotten. The broom of the domestic servant may as truly be used for God as was the sceptre of David or Solomon. You may have the humblest home and yet it may

be more resplendent with the glory of an indwelling
Christ than was the Temple in all its grandeur. The
hod-carrier's ladder may be trodden by angels' feet
as truly as was the ladder in the vision of Jacob.
We are all familiar with Herbert's admirable expression of this thought:

> "A servant with this clause
> Makes drudgery divine:
> Who sweeps a room, as for thy laws,
> Makes that and the action fine."

How Men May Honor the Lord.

Let us not think that we must do some great thing,
as we call it, to honor God; but let the little things
of life be done with a great motive, and God will be
honored. It is just as much the duty of some men
to make money as it is the duty of other men to
preach the Gospel. This thought is sublime—it is
divine. There are business men in this city who
are as consecrated to God as they are devoted to and
successful in business. They are an honor to the
Church of God and to the American Republic. For
such men I have a profound regard; they are true
ministers of Jesus Christ. God multiply their number!

There are men in the legal and medical professions
who use all their skill with this exalted motive.
There are mechanics to whom belongs this high meed

of praise; there are literary workers whose inspiration is the love of truth and Christ. These are the men who bless and save the world. If our daily duties be done in this spirit the workman's apron will be as holy as the bishop's robe; every hearth will be, in its measure, an altar to God; every home a house of God, and every meal a table of the Lord. Religion must make its power felt as truly in the marts of trade as in the sanctuary of God. Quaintly and truly has it been said:

> "In laborer's ballad oft more piety
> God finds, than in Te Deum's melody."

If all these things be true, then no man in health has a right to give up business. He may have money enough for himself, but the Lord's cause needs and demands all that he can make and bestow. But is it possible for the merchant, the doctor, the artist, the editor, the lawyer, the laborer, the preacher, to have distinctly before his mind at every moment God's glory as the lofty motive of his life? Perhaps not. I start for Boston; the train winds and turns; at some particular moment I may not seem to be going in the right direction. But I know that this is the Boston train, and I am sure that it will reach that city. So let a man know, in the bottom of his soul, that the dominant purpose, the controlling motive of his life, is to glorify God, then let him throw him-

self with the utmost enthusiasm into his work, and he
will not fail of securing the end which thus he seeks.
We have lost much in our daily duties, because we
have not carried into them this religious spirit.
Every obligation which rests upon a minister to
glorify God in his work rests upon all the members
of the Church to glorify him in their spheres of ac-
tivity.

But some of you business men are not Christians.
You ought to be. Christ demands that all your
powers be consecrated to his service; he demands
that you recognize him as the head of your firm.
he has a right to the proceeds of every transaction.
You are guilty in the sight of high heaven if, in carrying on your business, you fail to consult its true
head. You are dishonest if you use funds which
belong to another, and give him neither an ac-
counting nor a recognition. Bring your business,
your profession, your heart to-day to Jesus Christ.
Give him yourself. Give him all you have and
are. This is his right. This is your duty and
privilege.

God is to be Glorified in Our Social Life.

In our social life God is to be glorified. This opens
a wide domain. Here woman reigns as queen. Her
power is regnant for good or evil. In these later
days Christian women have come into positions of

prominence and power. It is a serious thing when women are found to glorify a bad fashion rather than to glorify God. Many a young man has blighted his life whose first wrong step was taken when the wine-cup was given him by some fair but foolish woman. So, too, many a man has been saved to Christ and the Church by the influences thrown around him in a Christian home. There are homes whose atmosphere is like that of heaven. Women, make the circle in which you move feel the power of Christian love. Young women, you especially exercise a power greater than you know; as you love Christ, as you love all that Christ loves, use that power to glorify God and to draw all about you to higher and holier lives.

Our recreations and amusements also should glorify God. Our whole lives may be a liturgy; every obligation an inspiration, and every duty a sacrament. No religious teacher can specify the amusements in which a Christian may safely share. But there are general principles which we can apply. Whatever lessens one's influence as a Christian man, whatever keeps him from honestly and successfully confessing Christ, whatever interrupts his loving intercourse with his Saviour, whatever prevents him from glorifying God—that he must abandon, if it were dear as a right hand or an eye. Social position, literary culture, beauty, and accomplishments of every kind are to be laid joyously at Jesus' feet. His service sweetens and ennobles every attainment; and every attainment, all true art, all forms of beauty and culture, may be so used as to add to the lustre of his glorious name.

Terrible was this charge, and delivered in solemn tone: "The God in whose hand thy breath is, and whose are all thy ways, hast thou not glorified." When the Church shall live for God alone, when her meat and drink shall be to do his will, then, indeed, shall she be "fair as the moon, clear as the sun, and terrible as an army with banners."

IX.

Marital Piety.

THIS striking and beautiful statement is made of Zacharias and his wife, Elizabeth. Both husband and wife had significant names: Zacharias means whom Jehovah remembers, and Elizabeth means God's oath or worshipper. When the sacerdotal families became numerous, David divided them into twenty-four classes. Of course so large a number of priests could not officiate at one time at the Tabernacle or the Temple. It was, therefore, arranged that each course should serve a week or eight days, from Sabbath to Sabbath, and the eighth in the order of the twenty-four classes was the course of Abia, or rather Abijah. The heads of these twenty-four courses were chief priests, and were also members of the Sanhedrim. A priest might marry into any one of the tribes, but both Zacharias and his wife were of the house of Aaron. This fact made their offspring the more illustrious among the Jews. Priestly rank was an indication of family greatness. John the Baptist was thus nobly descended: his father was a priest and his mother was of the daughters of Aaron. Thus by both father and mother he descended from the family of Amram; and from this family came also Moses, Aaron, and Miriam, than whom there were no more illustrious characters in the long line of Jewish history. This interesting couple thus rejoiced in a great ancestry; they also, by the special favor of God, became the parents of a famous son, and they were themselves worthy in their own characters alike of their distinguished ancestors and their famous descendant. Let us notice some of the characteristics of their piety as they are brought out in the text.

1. Theirs was a genuine piety—"They were *righteous before God.*" These words give this couple a noble commendation. The Word of God does not hesitate to give the due meed of praise to genuine worth. The apostle Paul loved to give commendation. He did not hesitate to blame when blame was deserved, but to commend rather than to censure he greatly preferred. We must not suppose that this description of the priestly pair is intended to imply that they were sinless. There is no suggestion here of sinlessness in heart or life; but there is

a strong affirmation of general conformity to the
law of God. Their righteousness was not like that
of the Pharisee, merely outward and before men, but
it was before the Omniscient God. They were sin-
cerely pious within and without. The reference is
especially to their strict observance of the law, as is
afterward implied. Doubtless there was an acknowl-
edgment of sin by them when it was committed,
and a hearty striving against the repetition of the
sinful act or thought. It is a high commendation,
indeed, that the inspired writer gave them when he
affirms that they were righteous before God. It
is possible for us to deceive ourselves. Rebekah
deceived herself and then her aged husband. The
Jesuitical saying, that the end justifies the means,
victimizes the Jesuit himself before he is able by
it to victimize others. We impose upon ourselves
before we impose upon our fellow-men. We must be
untrue to our own nature before we can be untrue to
those about us. The great dramatist teaches a profound philosophy when he exhorts us first to be true
to ourselves, and assures us that then we cannot be
false to any man. The hypocrite makes himself his
first victim. It is possible for us also for a time to
deceive those about us. I have read of a London
artist who exhibited a painting representing a friar
clothed in his canonicals. When viewed at a distance the painting seemed to represent the friar

devoutly engaged in prayer. Across his breast his hands are clasped together; like the publican in the parable, he does not look up to the place where God's honor dwells. Indeed, he seems to be so absorbed in his devotion and so earnest in his adoration as to arrest attention and excite admiration; but as the onlooker draws nearer the deception vanishes. What at a distance seemed to be a prayer-book is now discovered to be a punch-bowl. The hypocrite's hands are not across his breast in the attitude of devotion, but only in the act of squeezing a lemon. This quaint idea is a striking illustration of a hypocrite. Doubtless this picture fairly sets forth the lives of too many who are righteous before men but not righteous before God. They cannot long escape detection. No man can long play the hypocrite. What is in every man will surely come out. Give a man time enough and he will reveal his true character. Self-revelation is inevitable in the life of every responsible being. The acts of a man's life will assuredly reveal the thoughts of his heart. Prolonged imposition is an utter impossibility. The great God looks through all human subterfuges and attempted hypocrisies. All things are naked and opened unto his eye. We cannot deceive God. Glorious, then, is the inspired commendation that this beautiful couple " were righteous before God."

2. Theirs was a mutual piety—" They were *both*

righteous before God." They were not unequally
yoked together; their harmony in their religious
faith was a signal mercy to both. It is a blessed
thing when those who are joined together in marriage are also joined together in Christian experience
by both being joined to the Lord. It is difficult to
understand how a woman who has given her heart
to the Lord Jesus can really give her hand to a man
who rejects the Lord Jesus. It is difficult to see
how she can be loyal to her Lord and be loving
toward a man who hates that Lord. How can light
have fellowship with darkness? A man who is
struggling heavenward, while his wife lives for this
life alone, is like a bird trying to fly with but one
wing. It is impossible that a man and a woman
united in the bonds of matrimony should not influence each other for good or for evil. The Cherokee
marriage ceremony beautifully expresses the unity of
thought and life which should characterize the marriage relation. It is said that among this people the
man and woman join hands in marriage over running water, to indicate that henceforth their lives
are to flow in one unbroken stream. A good wife is
one of heaven's choicest gifts to man; she is God's
angel of mercy; and she may be man's daily guar-
dian and constant benediction. Abraham and Sarah
were right in their anxiety regarding the wife that
Isaac should choose; and every parent should mani-

fest a similar and, justifiable solicitude. The marriage relation is profoundly solemn. We do not forget the proverb which says that in marriage "you tie a knot with your tongue that you cannot untie with your teeth." It is a knot which should not be hastily tied, and which should never be untied except by the hand of death. As the years of pastoral life pass, I come more and more to attach importance to this relationship. Christian young men and young women should seek God's guidance and approval in every step which they take, and in every bond into which they enter. Some who once were active in the Christian life soon after marriage show as little interest in religious things as if they had been buried instead of being married. Christian wife, stand true to your religious obligations, even if your husband should laugh or sneer. Bring up your children in the fear of God. Ask God's blessing at your table. Erect the family altar in your home; rather live in a roofless house than in a prayerless home. Mothers may control family life and train their children for good and for God even when fathers are comparatively indifferent to both. Christian father, if your wife be not a child of God still stand firm in your faith and loyally discharge your duty. Your wife as a prayerless mother is a sight which might make angels weep; but you may be able by God's grace so to live as to train your children aright even though her influence be negatively, religious or openly irreligious. But it must be said that a man assumes a tremendous risk in marrying a woman of this kind. God grant that husbands and wives, united in all the other relations of life, may walk together in the narrow path which leads to heaven.

3. Theirs was a practical piety—"*walking* in all the commandments and ordinances of the Lord blameless." Walking is that movement of the body by which it changes its place and performs its daily duty. In the Christian life this act stands for the trend, the tendency, the actuality, the totality of life. When it is said that Enoch walked with God, we have a comprehensive statement of the controlling motive and practical characteristic of his entire life. Our religion must be one which manifests itself in our daily walk and conversation. Like the vestal fire, it must be a light which is never extinguished. There is an irressitible power in such a religion. You can no more lessen its influence by opposition than you can blot out the sun by denying its existence. Quaintly has it been said that the Christian has first to make a good profession and then he has to make his profession good. Ten men read a Christian's life for every man who reads the Christian's Bible. A Christian should be a living witness for God; he should be an incarnation of God's thought, of purity of heart, nobility of life, and Christliness of

character. Elijah, in connection with Ahab, was a witness for the God of Israel whose testimony could neither be silenced nor misunderstood. Joseph in Egypt, resisting temptation because he would not sin against God, bore a testimony mightier than a whole library on the evidences of religion. Daniel in Babylon could still be loyal to God and faithful in the performance of duty. True religion must consist not only in joyous emotion, but chiefly in constant faithfulness to duty, and in consistent obedience to God. True religion enables a man to control his thoughts, to ennoble his speech, and to purify his life. True religion makes a man a gentleman in the noble sense of that word; it makes a man honest in business life; it makes a man true in all his relations to his fellow-men always and everywhere. It goes with him wherever he goes. In this sense we need a walking religion. The man who can hide his religion has a religion not worth hiding. The soldier who will not wear his regimentals is no soldier. A banner is to be displayed; only as it is displayed, is it a banner; and God has given us a banner that it should be displayed for the truth. True religion makes a man give the right number of ounces to the pound, of inches to the yard, and of cents to the dollar. It makes him the greatest and noblest representative of God upon this sinful earth. This was the religion possessed by this noble couple of that

olden time.   This is the religion which every man
and woman, every boy and girl, ought to possess and
to manifest in our day.

4. Theirs was an *impartial* piety—" They walked
in *all* the commandments and ordinances of the Lord
blameless." By the commandments here we are to
understand not only the ceremonial rites and ordinances, but also the moral requirements, of the law.
The word ordinances stands specially for ceremonial
observances.   Although they were of the priestly
order, they were not satisfied with a mere ritual religion; they could not find peace in mere external
compliance with the divine requirements.   They
discovered the inner, the deeper, the spiritual meaning of God's law. There never was but one true religion.   Its fundamental principles are the same in all
climes and centuries.   Christ came not to destroy
but to fulfil the law.   The first commandment of the
decalogue he acknowledged in his summary of the
law; and he nowhere contradicts any of the teachings of the decalogue.   The man in our day who
will truly strive to keep the first commandment of
the ten will be led to the feet and to the heart of
Jesus Christ.

There was no partiality in the faith of this noble
husband and wife for one table of the law over the
other.   Like the Lord's Prayer, the first part of the
decalogue refers to God and to our duty to him; but

the second table refers to our duty to our fellow-men. In the Lord's Prayer we are taught to pray that God's name may be hallowed and his will be done, before we pray for daily bread and the forgiveness of our debts; but the two parts of this prayer, like the two parts of the decalogue, stand in closest relation. To keep either table of the law aright implies the keeping of both tables aright. It has been said of some people that they are very pious Godward, but very "shaky" manward. Wherever this statement can truly be made a severe criticism is pronounced. If we do not love our fellow-men whom we have seen, how can we show that we love God whom we have not seen? Love to God must show itself by love to our neighbor. If we try to live on one table of the decalogue, or on one part of the Lord's Prayer, we become like a boat with one oar or a bird with one wing. If the hand be outstretched in supplication toward God, it must also be opened in benefaction toward men. There is great danger of partiality in our choice of God's commandments. Many a man practically says: "This commandment harmonizes with my taste; therefore, I shall perform it. That one does not; therefore, I shall neglect it. This one is in line with my social relations; that one is not. I shall obey the one and neglect the other. This one is essential to salvation; I shall perform it. That one is not; therefore, I shall neglect it." Such an atti-

9

tude as this is unworthy of a true Christian man.
He never asks, how little can I do and be saved; he
simply inquires, "Lord, what wilt thou have me to
do?" Our Lord instructed his apostles to teach
those whom they discipled to observe all things whatsoever he had commanded. Belief, baptism, all
things that Christ commands, are necessary to obedience. Christ stated the true test of love to be
obedience. His words are, "If a man love me he will
keep my words." The spirit of obedience, as shown
by this consecrated pair, should be the spirit of every
heart now as then.

5. Theirs was a blameless piety—"walking in.all
the commandments and ordinances of the Lord
blameless." This does not mean that they were sinless; verse twenty of this chapter clearly shows that
they were not sinless. Zacharias was guilty of
unbelief, but this commendation shows that they
were exemplary observers of God's law. It also
teaches us that their character was irreproachable,
and that they would not knowingly and willingly
indulge in sin. Doubtless they strove to have con-
sciences void of offence toward God and toward man.
We cannot always be without blame. If we have
positive elements in our character we will provoke
antagonism and arouse hostility. As far as possible
we are to live peaceably with all men and in the

enjoyment of the reputation of being "blameless and harmless, the sons of God, without rebuke." It will not, however, be possible always so to live as to escape sharp criticism. We may, however, live lives of such transparent sincerity as to make opposition powerless, and the arrows of criticism pointless. Beautiful is the prayer of the apostle for the Philippians, when he prays that "Ye may be sincere and without offence." This prayer implies that they would not willingly injure others in property or in reputation. The word translated sincere in this connection is an unusually suggestive one. The word sincere is not the exact translation, but it also is worthy of our thought; it means "without wax," and is applied to honey which is pure and transparent, or to furniture which is without cracks and knot-holes filled with wax. This is a beautiful description of Christian character. But, as already noted, the word sincere does not correctly translate the original word in this prayer on behalf of the Philippians. The Greek word properly means that which is judged of in the sunshine. An article in a dark room may appear flawless and perfect, but when exposed to bright sunshine its defects will appear. This is a prayer that a Christian's life may be so perfect that it may be judged in the brightest sunshine of daily publicity. Sincerity of this character means far more than the mere absence of criticism; it has its positive elements, but when a life is thus sincere it will soon disarm hostile criticism, and will soon compel general respect and appreciation.

How can such a life be lived? How may such a religious character as this ancient couple possessed be secured? These are reasonable and practical questions. There. is but one perfect life, the life of the Lord Jesus. Once only did the plant of humanity blossom and bloom into a perfect flower; but, with our perverted taste and sinful natures, we cannot imitate that perfect life without renovation, without re-creation, without conversion, without regeneration. We must bring our soiled lives and our tainted hearts to God that both may be washed and made white in the fountain of cleansing. We must go to Christ just as we are, that we may be made as he would have us. Accept Jesus Christ now. Throw wide open the doors of the heart to his entrance. He will come as your heavenly guest. He will expel unholy thoughts and control unrighteous acts. He will purify the very fountain of life within, and, as the streams flow out in words and acts, they will be wholesome and become purifying like the fountain itself. Then old things shall have passed away, and all things shall have become new. Then shall we be new creatures in Christ Jesus, and by his grace we shall be able, like Zacharias and Elizabeth, to walk in all the commandments and ordinances of the Lord blameless; and then at the last we shall be presented before him and be blameless in his sight.

X.

Four Great Things.

"And an angel of the Lord came up from Gilgal to Bochim, and said, I made you to go out of Egypt, and have brought you unto the land which I sware unto your fathers; and I said, I will never break my covenant with you. And ye shall make no league with the inhabitants of this land; ye shall throw down their altars : but ye have not obeyed my voice. Why have ye done this ?

" Wherefore I also said, I will not drive them out from before you; but they shall be as thorns in your sides, and their gods shall be a snare unto you.

" And it came to pass, when the angel of the Lord spake these words unto all the children of Israel, that the people lifted up their voice and wept.

_" And they called the name of that place Bochim: and they sacrificed there unto the Lord."—_JUDGES ii. 1-5.

WE have in the previous chapter an account of several important matters which occurred shortly after the death of Joshua. In the chapter from which the text is taken, we have an account of those men who were the contemporaries of Joshua when they had, to a considerable degree, forsaken

God, and were, as a result, without his special presence and blessing. When they forsook God they became subject to the Canaanites; having broken their covenant with God, they made it impossible for him to fulfil his promises to grant them his leadership and to give them power over their foes. This chapter, and the first eight verses of the next, give us in brief space the substance of the whole Book of Judges. We here see the sad results of the sin committed by God's people in their loss of power and in the absence of the divine presence. We also have an account of the repentance of the people, of God's pardoning mercy, and finally of his deliverance of them out of the hands of their enemies. This is the circle in which these historic events move, and this circle is practically that in which the whole history of Israel and of the entire Church continually revolves. Coming immediately to the text, we have as the topic of this discourse Four Great Things:

1. The first of these four is a Great Preacher. This great preacher is called in the first verse "an angel of the Lord;" it is also said that he "came up from Gilgal to Bochim." The question at once arises, Who was this great preacher? To that question many answers have been given. The Targum calls him a prophet; some modern interpreters also adopt this view, adding that he was endowed by God with extraordinary powers for carrying out an extraordi-

nary commission. Great duties, it is certain, were
laid upon this preacher, as he had to rebuke the
people for their sins and to explain why God had not
driven out his and their enemies from the land which
he had bestowed upon his people. Some Jewish commentators and others believe that this preacher was
Phinehas, the high-priest. They reason that a man
must be meant, because he is said to come from a
place in the land and not from heaven, because he
addressed a congregation of the people, and because
he is not described as disappearing from their sight.
Others understand this preacher to be an angel, in
the ordinary meaning of that term. There are, however, it seems to me, some serious, if not insuperable,
difficulties in these interpretations. It seems impossible that this preacher could have been a man or a
created angel. It is much more likely that he was
the same glorious personage who is often spoken of
in the Scriptures as the Angel of the Covenant. The
same who met Abraham, the father of the faithful,
with whom he entered into fraternal and heavenly
communion; the same who warned Lot to flee from
Sodom; the same august being who met and
wrestled with the patriarch Jacob on the banks of
the brook Jabbok; the same who appeared to Moses
in the burning bush; the same who brought Israel
with an high hand and an outstretched arm out of
Egypt, who led the great host through the wilderness

and finally into the land of Canaan; the same who appeared so mysteriously and sublimely to Joshua as the captain of the Lord's hosts near Gilgal; and the same who appeared to Gideon when threshing wheat with a flail in the wine-press. It is distinctly said, in this latter connection, "Jehovah looked upon him and said, Go in this thy might." This interpretation makes this great preacher no less and no other than the Lord Jesus Christ. The Son of God honored the world with frequent temporary incarnations before he became the child of Mary in the manger of Bethlehem. The Jehovah of the Old Testament is certainly the Jesus of the New Testament. There is almost no doubt that in this case this was a divine messenger from heaven. During the period of Israel's history covered by the Book of Judges, the visits of angels were more frequent than was formerly or subsequently the case, and there were reasons for these more frequent visits during that period. The records of their appearances belong, in a marked degree, to the period of the Judges and to that of the Captivity. It is well known that these were transition periods in the history of God's people; the period of the Judges was destitute of prophetic guidance and of certain former elements of direct revelation. It was, therefore, fitting that extraordinary messengers, created angels, and even the uncreated Angel of the Covenant, should come with messages from the throne of Israel's King. During the period of the Captivity Israel was brought into peculiar trials because of unusual contact with heathenism; it was, therefore, fitting that during that period also special manifestations of God's will should be given by the visits of angels.

This great preacher was sent to God's thoughtless people at this time to secure their attention and to preserve them from idolatry and so from destruction. Two reasons make it clear that this was neither a man nor a created angel. He does not use the ordinary formula of delegated authority; he does not speak in the name of the Lord; he does not say, "Thus saith the Lord;" and again he ascribes to himself the honor of bringing the children of Israel out of Egypt, and he makes a covenant with them and threatens them with punishment if they do not turn from their sin. Who but God could use language of this sort? Who but God might say, "I made you to go up out of Egypt," and "have brought you into the land which I sware unto your fathers." We know that a little time before Joshua had warned the people against entangling alliances with the Canaanites, but these warnings they wickedly rejected. Now a greater than Joshua, the true Joshua, Jehovah-Jesus, repeats these solemn warnings. Like their descendants long years after, they despised the servants of God; but of them as of those to whom Christ spoke, we may say, perhaps they will reverence the Son. We are here told that this great preacher came from Gilgal, and it has been suggested that perhaps the journey was made flying swiftly, as the angel Gabriel came to Daniel. It is natural that Gilgal should be mentioned in this connection. It had long been the headquarters of the people of Israel after they reached Canaan; in Gilgal God had shown them many and great favors, and there the covenant of circumcision had been renewed. The fact that this great preacher came from Gilgal would add force to his words; the mention of this place would remind them of their solemn but now slighted obligations. It was well for them, and it is well for us, to be reminded of the solemn vows which certain places and periods in our history suggest and emphasize.

It is a wonderfully inspiring thought that we have a visit and a sermon from the Lord Jesus in this early day, and that the account of both is given in this ancient record. We are accustomed to associate the preaching of Christ with the Sermon on the Mount; but here is a sermon from the Divine Preacher recorded in the Book of Judges. Of this earlier, and of the later, sermon we can say: "Never man spake like this man." Jesus Christ is still the world's Great Preacher. Our most eloquent preachers are but voices telling of his name and glory; their highest honor is to point to him and say: "Behold the Lamb of God, which taketh away the sin of the world." This Great Preacher still comes to the assemblies of God's people. He is here this morning speaking words of awful authority, of sublime simplicity, and of tearful tenderness. He is here uttering his solemn warnings and pronouncing his precious promises. If the word shall be properly spoken in this pulpit this morning, not your pastor, but your Lord and Redeemer, is the preacher. Oh, listen, I beseech you, to this Divine Preacher and obey his heavenly message! Slight me and my words, but devoutly listen to my Lord, and bow in sweet submission at his feet.

2. A great congregation is next brought to our view. We know that a great congregation was assembled on this solemn and sublime occasion, for we learn from the fourth verse that "all the children of Israel" were present to hear the great preacher. It was fitting that so great a preacher should have a great congregation. We do not know with certainty why the whole people were thus assembled. The occasion may have been one of the three solemn feasts, when all the males of the children of Israel appeared at the Tabernacle of the Lord; or it may have been a solemn convocation of all the tribes to inquire of the Lord why they were not able to drive out the Canaanites; and it has even been suggested

that the people were assembled to complete their preparations for war. They had suffered much, and they may have determined now to unite their forces and to make a tremendous onset on their foes. It seems more likely, however, that they were met for worship rather than for war. The place of their assembly may have been Shiloh, where was the Tabernacle of the Lord. We know that the place was afterward called Bochim, a name which signifies weepers, because of the general lamentation of the people at this time; but probably the original name was Shiloh. The new name was given to the place because of the profound effect produced by this sermon. All Israel needed sharp reproof, and sharp reproof was now given and was received in the right spirit. Great congregations are desirable if they be properly secured. We know that congregations are to be weighed as well as counted; we know that some preachers "fit audiences find, though few;" we know that preachers are not to be judged either as to their ability or usefulness by the size of their audiences; we know that some of the great authors and preachers have spoken to small audiences, and we know that in our day the newspapers furnish the larger audiences for political orators and religious teachers. It is well understood that many a man, speaking in the halls of legislation of the state or the nation, is comparatively indifferent as to the size or interest of the audience before him; for he is speaking to his constituents perhaps in a distant part of the country, who will eagerly read his words as reported in the newspapers. The newspaper is to a great degree the flying angel with the roll in the nineteenth century. The advantages which the press offers to a preacher in enlarging the circle of his hearers are not to be despised, but to be constantly and earnestly used. Every preacher ought to seek for as large an audience as can legitimately be secured. If he has truths to present which fifty people ought to hear, they ought to be heard by five hundred, and, if possible, by five thousand. But no preacher is justified in using means unbecoming the dignity of his pulpit and the sacredness of his message in order to increase the number of his hearers; no preacher must dishonor himself by buffoonery or his message by misrepresentation in order to preach to great congregations. If a man chooses to resort to such unworthy means he can secure the crowd, and then can exert himself "to split the ears of the groundlings." But all such efforts are unworthy of him and are dishonoring to the Gospel and to the Lord. Audiences which begin by laughing with a clownish preacher will end, as the Autocrat of the Breakfast Table has suggested, by laughing at him. The motive which influences a preacher at all these points will give direction to the efforts which he makes.

It is very probable that we have not used the press and certain permissible pulpit methods to so great a degree as we might and ought. Preachers who take great pains thoroughly to prepare themselves often feel utterly discouraged because corresponding pains are not taken by even their own church-members to hear the words thus carefully prepared and earnestly spoken. Every preacher may well believe that he is not called upon to preach to empty seats. Empty seats do not need sermons. Church cushions have no souls either to be saved or lost. A former pastor in this city used to affirm that he had poured a sufficient amount of biblical knowledge and theological learning into the cushions on the back pews of his church to edify several theological seminaries, and a score of churches. We must not, however, neglect the audiences made up of one, two, or three. To Nicodemus, in that remarkable nocturnal interview, our blessed Lord poured out his heart with a glorious fulness and freeness of heavenly love; to this one hearer he gave a fuller statement of the part which each Person in the divine Trinity performs in the work of human redemption than is found anywhere else in the gospels or anywhere in the epistles. To the woman of Samaria at the well the Lord Jesus preached a wonderful sermon, and to this audience of one he gave the fullest declaration of his Messiahship that he had anywhere given up to

that time. As we read that declaration we are filled
with amazement alike at his condescension and wisdom. To the two disciples on the way to Emmaus
on the evening of his glorious resurrection-day, the
Lord Jesus gave more time than to any other persons, so far as the record goes, during the entire
period of the forty days between his resurrection and
his ascension. To these men he opened in a wonderful way the Old Testament Scriptures; to them
he gave the marvellous exposition of Moses and of
the prophets, showing how they spoke of himself,
and thus he made the hearts of the disciples burn
within them as he opened to them the Scriptures,
and opened also their eyes to behold wondrous things
therein. We need in our personal relations, both
as ministers and laymen, to make more of audiences
of one. We know that two or three is a gospel
quorum, and when they meet together they may be
assured that Christ will be in the midst. It is a
comparatively easy thing to denounce sin and sinners, not having any particular sin or sinner in mind;
but it is a very different thing to take a man by the
hand, to look him in the eyes, and say to him,
"Thou art the man," or thus personally to invite him
to yield his heart to God. Let us secure the largest
audiences we can by the use of proper means, and
then let us as ministers and laymen follow up the
public proclamation of truth by warm, hearty, per-

sonal appeals. Personal work for Christ is one of the possible glories of the Church, and one of the triumphs of its individual disciples. We can rightly imitate the example of Christ in preaching, when we may, to the great congregation, and in enforcing truth as we ought upon a single hearer.

3. We have here also a great sermon. It was not a long sermon, but it contained great truths and it produced remarkable results. That is always the best sermon, whatever its homiletic construction may be, which brings forth the most and the best fruit. The Lord's sermon on this occasion cut the people to the quick; like the apostle Peter's hearers on the day of Pentecost, "they were pricked in their heart." The great preacher reminded them of what God had done for them in bringing them out of the land of slavery and into the land of freedom and prosperity. With true oratorical skill he painted their former misery as a dark background on which he limned their present felicity. He contrasted in a striking way their former darkness with their present brightness, their previous devotion to national death with their present election to national life. He reminded them of his oath to their fathers, and of his promise that he would never break his covenant. That covenant he had not broken; if ever it were broken the fault would be theirs and not his. We make God's covenant null and void because we fail to perform our

10

part of the same. This divine preacher then proceeds to remind the people of what he had a right to expect from them in their relations to the Canaanites. They must not make a league with his enemies and theirs; they cannot serve God and the gods of the Canaanites. Here we have the announcement of great principles—principles which are as true to-day as they were in that day. The line of demarcation between the world and the Church should be broad and deep. We must not attempt to play fast and loose with the commands of God; there must be no halting on our part between the claims of the world and the rights of God. God has no need of half-hearted professors of religion; the lukewarm he rejects with a holy loathing: he would have us either cold or hot. This great sermon further shows that the people had disobeyed God in all his commands and ordinances; they forgot their covenant with the Most High, and made leagues with the Canaanites; they neglected God's altar, and did not throw down the altars of his and their foes. This sermon, then, demands that they shall give an explanation for their disobedience. What excuse is possible for their misconduct? How can they make an apology for their opposition to the truth and their fellowship with sin and sinners? But are not we guilty as were they? Are there not those in this audience who in like manner have forgotten God, and who have worshipped Belial rather than God; who have neglected divine duties and have given time, thought, and earnest service to the works of darkness? While we pronounce a right judgment on these great sinners, shall we not also willingly and penitently admit that we are also in the same condemnation?

But as we study this ancient sermon by our Lord, we see also that his hearers and we must expect to suffer for neglect of duty and commission of evil. Our Lord here shows that, because of the sin of the people, he refuses to drive out the Canaanites; this truth is earnestly taught in the third verse of my text. The Lord practically says, "You will not obey my commands, therefore I will not fulfil my promises." Here also a great law in the divine economy and in human experience is declared. If we indulge in sin, we forfeit the grace of God; if we do not resist the devil, God will not trample him under our feet. There is no possibility of escaping the action of these great moral forces which sweep through the universe. The Lord further declares here that the Canaanites shall be as thorns in the sides of the Israelites, and the gods of the heathen shall be a snare to his people. This is an illustration of the inevitable tendency of evil. The law of addition has its full manifestation when we yield to the first sin; sins multiply with fearful rapidity. One lie necessitates a hundred. There is a gracious

law of addition in Christian experience; for while
one man of God shall chase a thousand men of the
devil, two men of God shall chase not two thousand,
but ten thousand, disciples of Satan. This gracious
principle has its sad illustration when the law of
addition is perverted to the service of sin and Satan.
The men who trifle with sin shall be triumphed over
by evil; "whatsoever a man soweth, that shall he
also reap." This law is universal as gravitation,
and eternal as God.

4. We have here also a great result. To this
point every sermon ought to tend. Sermons are not
ends, but means to ends. We do not preach to save
sermons, but to save souls. It is said that when
Massillon preached at Versailles, Louis XIV. paid
a tribute to the power of his sermons which every
preacher might well covet. The haughty king, after
hearing one of Massillon's powerful appeals to the
conscience, said: "Father, when I hear some men
preach I go away saying, How eloquent the preacher
is! But when I hear you, I go away saying, How
great a sinner I am!" This remark gives us an
important distinction between two kinds of preaching, and pronounces a fine encomium on the latter
method. When we turn to the fourth verse of my text,
we read of this great congregation that "the people
lifted up their voices and wept." The arrow of divine
truth went through the joints of their harness and

pierced the heart. Like the publican, they were ready
to beat upon their breasts and each one say: "God be
merciful to me a sinner!" Like some of those who beheld the Great Preacher of this occasion afterward upon the cross, they were ready to mourn as one mourn-
eth for his first-born. Doubtless they feared God's
wrath; they knew well that they had merited his
righteous indignation. As a result of their weepings,
the place, as we have seen, was called Bochim. Disobedience to God will always bring tears when our
guilt is realized. We read also that they offered
sacrifices unto Jehovah at the close of this sermon;
they thus desired to atone for the sins of which they
had been guilty. They thus acknowledged their sin,
and expressed a desire to comply with the appointments of God in the case of sinners.

Ought there not to be weeping over sin in this
audience this morning? Have we joined in denunciation of the guilt of this ancient audience while
listening to the Divine Preacher? Shall we dare go
to our homes now without joining them in weeping
for our own sins as they did for theirs? We have
sinned against greater light. They were in the gray
dawn of the morning; we are in the brightness of
its noonday sun. They saw Christ's day at best afar
off; we have stood beside his cross hearing his dying
groan, and we have seen him go forth in triumph
from the tomb uttering his triumphant "All hail!"

They had to offer sacrifices for their sin, but the great sacrifice has now been offered once for all. We have now but to accept its gracious provisions; we have now but to give ourselves as living sacrifices unto God. Let your pastor disappear from view; let the Angel of the Covenant, Jehovah-Jesus, be the preacher this morning. Listen now to his voice as he says to each one: "My son, my daughter, give me thine heart;" and let your sweet response be:

"Here's my heart—oh, take and seal it!
Seal it for thy courts above!"

XI.

The Old Testament Unfolded in the New.

"And beginning at Moses, and all the prophets, he expound-ed unto them in all the Scriptures the things concerning him-self."—LUKE xxiv. 27.

THE Bible is not two books, but one. There never were two true religions in the world, but only one. Judaism and Christianity, when both are rightly understood, teach the same great truth, and are in perfect harmony with each other. Judaism is the root and the trunk; Christianity is the flower and the fruit. Judaism is the gray dawn of the morning; Christianity is the sunshine in its noonday splendor. The apostle Paul was never opposed to Christianity in the philological meaning of that word. The devout men on the day of Pentecost were really not opposed to Christianity. The apostle Paul and these "devout men out of every nation under heaven" were Messiahians, if we may coin a new word. They believed in and they loved the

Messiah, but they did not know that Jesus of Nazareth was the Messiah of prophecy. When the apostle
Paul learned this truth he cried out, "Lord, what
wilt thou have me to do?" When these men, on the
day of Pentecost, learned this truth they said,
"Men and brethren, what shall we do?" Messiahians
are Christians. The one word is Hebrew, the other
is Greek, but both mean the same thing. A devout
Jew needed only to know that Jesus was the Christ
to believe in him, and thus to become a true Jew by
being a true Christian. He is not a true Jew who
is only a Jew; he is the true Jew who has passed
from Judaism into Christianity. There is no contradiction between these two forms of faith. The
one is the germ, the other the fruit; the one is childhood, the other is manhood; the one, as we have
already implied, is morning, the other is noonday.
There is no contradiction between the law and the
Gospel. The law is the Gospel implied, suggested,
foreshadowed; the Gospel is the law realized,
actualized, fulfilled. Finely did Augustine long ago
say: "The New Testament is enfolded in the Old,
and the Old Testament is unfolded in the New."

1. We might expect that the New Testament
would unfold the Old when we consider what is the
design of both Testaments. If we discover clearly
what this design is we shall see clearly that there
must be harmony between both, and that the later

Testament must reveal and glorify the earlier. The design of the Bible is to make known God and men in their mutual relations; it is to manifest God's fulness and man's need; it is to supply man's spiritual necessities discovered by the recognition of these mutual relations. Many mistake the true design of the Word of God. They seem to think that it is a text-book of science, of history, and of systematic theology. Because they do not find all these and kindred subjects treated *in extenso*, they turn away from the book with disappointment and oppose it with unfairness. The Bible is not a text-book on any one of these subjects. It does, however, give us much information of the most valuable kind on all these subjects; but its references to history are always subordinate to the main design for which it was written.

Not Herodotus, but Moses, is the true Father of History. More than a thousand years before the days of Herodotus Moses earned the right to this title. The Bible also gives us frequent and beautiful descriptions of nature. It anticipated in no doubtful allusions many of the discoveries of scientists in most recent times: the circulation of the blood, the Copernican system of astronomy, and similar comparatively recent discoveries are certainly suggested in biblical statements. But all these allusions are merely incidental. God, in giving us a revelation of his will, was pleased to make the book, as Dr. Hamilton has said, attractive as well as instructive. He has filled it with sunny pictures, with charming incidents, with thrilling narratives, with stately arguments, and with lofty descriptions, while its main purpose was to guide us to purity of life and to faith in God as our Father and Saviour. Creation may show us God's hand, but revelation shows us God's heart. It reveals not only that he has an almighty arm, but also that he has a motherly heart. Apart from the Word of God, it is impossible for us rightly to understand the heart of God. It reveals to us at the same time the condition of man as a sinner and the necessity of his regeneration, that he may become truly a child of God. Even heathen mythology taught in some vague way these great truths. But the Bible throws a flood of brightest light where heathenism threw only the dark shadow of speculation.

The Bible also reveals our destiny, and declares the possibility of our being heirs of God and joint heirs with Jesus Christ; but the wisest sages of heathenism could only guess at these great truths. The Bible also clearly makes known the manner by which sinful men may receive the forgiveness and be admitted to the favor of God. In carrying out this lofty purpose the unity of both Testaments might fairly be assumed. The same lesson was given in the Old Testament as in the New; but in the Old Testament we spell it out in a dim alphabet, while in the New we pronounce it in letters of living light. God is one; truth is one. God cannot contradict himself. His voice in one age, in one dispensation, in one book, must harmonize with his voice in all ages, dispensations, and revelations. If the sun which is rising in the Old Testament be the Sun of Righteousness we may expect that it will shine in undimmed splendor in the noonday of the New Testament. God's love was declared even at the gates of Eden. Here floated out the first notes of that celestial song whose full chorus was heard on the plains of Bethlehem. God's love was shining in its dawning light along the whole line of Old Testament story, but it shone in its meridian splendor around the cross of his only-begotten Son, our well-beloved Redeemer.

2. We might expect that the New Testament would unfold the Old when we consider the necessity of unity in carrying out this grand design. There is apparently great diversity in the Bible. We find it divided into sixty-six tracts and into two great divisions. In the former division there are thirty-nine of these booklets, written by thirty-two different men, and in the latter twenty-seven written by eight different men. Thus not fewer than forty writers have been engaged in the preparation of the

entire volume. These writers represented various countries, nationalities, degrees of intelligence, social conditions, and religious attainments. Some of them were prophets, some priests, some kings; some were statesmen, some herdsmen, some farmers, some fishermen. To the careless reader these facts would imply a great lack of unity in the result. And this apparent lack would be the more marked when we observe the great variety there is in the contents of these sixty-six tracts. They contain histories of creation, of various institutions, of intricate laws, and of many persons; they contain biographies, poems, and prophecies. Some of them deal with the past and some with the future; some stretch forward to the grand consummation of all things in a new heaven and a new earth. But we have not here a meaningless and heterogeneous mass of facts. All these writings are but one book, and that book comes to us with claims of greater antiquity and of higher authority than any other volume known among men. It has excited more bitter hatred and it has evoked tenderer love than any other book. No man can study it prayerfully and profoundly without being impressed with its genuineness, authenticity, unity, and uniqueness. It was the production of men who wrote for immediate necessities, and yet it speaks for all climes and centuries. As it is the oldest, so it is the wisest, the most beautiful, and the most sublime of volumes. No one of the miracles which it narrates is half so miraculous as the narration itself. It is the founder of all schools of learning and the corner-stone of all true systems of civilization and the basis of all codes of law. It has inspired the loftiest poetry and the noblest music, the grandest literature, the most enduring painting, and the divinest sculpture.

This diversity is, however, in harmony with God's method in nature. The human body has many parts, but it is one body. No man can study its structure without discovering unity in its design. The wisdom of its Author is seen in the adjustment of its parts. Precisely so is it in creation as a whole. No man who carefully studies all the spheres of God's creative power can doubt for a moment that one thought dominates the whole. There is perfect unity in the midst of the greatest diversity; there is perfection even in the midst of apparent incompletion. The glory of any art or work is that it accomplishes the purpose of its creation. God's great Book of Nature is thus complete. It reveals his thoughts in rocks and flowers, in fields and forests. The heavens declare his glory and the song of birds is the chanting of his praise. He has made river and rivulet; and sea and ocean are revelations alike of his wisdom and power. All the discoveries of our own times go to prove the unity of creation. Each department of inquiry is but a fragment in itself, but all put together give us a grand and perfect whole. Sciences which were once supposed to stand widely apart are constantly tending, as modern investigation shows, to union. It has been well said by Principal Dawson, that "the great natural forces of light, heat, and electricity are tending to coalesce. The spectroscope has united optics and chemistry with one another and with astronomy. Geology has welded together in the past history of the earth a great number of physical sciences."

This great diversity is consistent with the highest forms of unity, human and divine. All great works must be characterized by unity. No poem can be truly called great except it possess this characteristic. While there is in the Bible a lack of any formal system of theology, there is present in glorious ful ness the great truths which God designs to communicate to men. System is human; method is divine. Perfect system we expect to find in cabinet and in herbarium; but we do not find it associated with living things. God has his own method of revelation. In the Bible there is the joyous variety of nature, but unity everywhere. The man who rightly studies it discovers in any particular book, or in the relation of that book to the other books, a unity as real as he finds in a Shakespearian play, in Milton's "Paradise Lost," or in Tennyson's "In

Memoriam." With all the variety necessarily in the histories, biographies, apothegms, poems, proverbs, prophecies, and moral discourses, there is a unity as real as that which we find in the human body—a unity as real as between foundation-walls and towers of some glorious temple. Mr. William Walters, in his book entitled "Claims of the Bible," illustrates this thought when he says: "We have a diversity of currents and streams, yet they all belong to the mighty river of Revelation—the river of the water of life, proceeding from the throne of God and the Lamb."

Growing out of this fact we see that one inspired writer quotes from another in support of his statements. We see that the epistles illustrate the Pentateuch, and the gospels unfold the prophecies. The great purpose for which the Bible was written is never forgotten from the first majestic words of Genesis to the last love-notes of Revelation. Finely has Mr. Beecher said: "As in Beethoven's matchless music there runs one idea, worked out through all the changes of measure and key, now almost hidden, now breaking out in rich natural melody, whispered in the treble, murmured in the bass, simply suggested in the prelude, but growing clearer and clearer as the work proceeds, winding gradually back until it ends in the key in which it began, and closes in triumphant harmony, so throughout the Bible there runs one great idea, man's ruin by sin and his redemption by grace—in a word, Jesus Christ the Saviour." This being true, we might expect that the Old Testament would enfold the New and the New Testament unfold the Old.

3. What we might expect we actually find as the result of a careful examination of the teaching of the New Testament. There is in the Word of God a true development from first to last. There is rhetorical skill in the revelations of God; he is the grand rhetorician, as he is the divine logician. The Bible might well be studied for its literary merits along the line of exact logic, as truly as in the great realm of its lyric poetry, or in its loftier strains of seraphic prophecy. There is in it the genuine progress of thought, which a true literary style demands and illustrates. It is no cold and mechanical production, but is a living organism, animated in every part by the breath of God.

As the oak is in the acorn, so was the New Testament in the Old. As the Corliss engine was once a thought in the mind of its inventor, so was the completed Testament in the mind of its divine Author. In Genesis we have the germ of all the revelations of God and man, of sin and redemption, found in the later portions of the Old Testament and in all portions of the New. Indeed, it is not possible to understand either Testament except as we understand both. The man who thinks he honors the New by dishonoring the Old has succeeded simply in dishonoring both. It is astounding that men should lightly esteem the earliest portions of this one revelation with some vague idea of giving thereby additional honor to the later portions of the same. As well might they think they honored the lofty crown of the Eiffel Tower while they attempted to destroy its deep foundation. Any man who will stand in the Book of Genesis at the gate of Eden will see the foundations of the grand structure whose cap-stone is laid by Christ and his apostles. He will hear the first notes of the song whose full hymn of praise is sung on lonely Patmos, with the music of the waves breaking on the rock-bound shore as its grand accompaniment. Our blessed Lord showed most clearly that the New Testament unfolds the Old. Without him the Bible is meaningless; without him earth is hopeless; without him heaven is charmless. Around his cradle and his cross all the ages have gathered.

When he said in John viii. 56, " Your father Abraham rejoiced to see my day : and he saw it, and was glad," he unfolded to those who heard his words and to all who read them, Genesis xxii. 13 and 14, when Abraham found the burnt-offering instead of his son Isaac and called the name of that place Jehovah-jireh. When he said, in the tenth

11

chapter of the same gospel, "I am the good shepherd," he unfolded the twenty-third Psalm, in which David sang the praise of that good shepherd. When he cried upon the cross, "My God, my God, why hast thou forsaken me?" he unfolded the twenty-second Psalm, in which David sang of his crucified Lord. In his triumphant resurrection and glorious ascension he unfolded the twenty-fourth Psalm, in which David enfolded these great truths in his lofty song. It is impossible to read the story of his birth without seeing how gloriously it unfolds Isaiah's description of him as the Child born, the Son given whose name was Wonderful, Counsellor, the Mighty God, the Everlasting Father, and the Prince of Peace. It is impossible to read the prayer of the apostle John in apocalyptic vision—"Even so, come, Lord Jesus"—without having suggested to our mind the long line of prophecies regarding that coming from the first announcement in Genesis iii. 15, that the seed of the woman should bruise the head of the serpent. It is not possible to walk with Christ on the way to Emmaus on the evening of his resurrection-day without seeing how gloriously he unfolded the Old Testament concerning himself. His words rebuke all who deny the harmony between the two Testaments and all who depreciate the value of the Old Testament. Our Lord gave more of his time on that day to these two travellers, Cleopas and the unknown, bo he evangelist Luke or some other disciple, than he gave to any other company, so far as we know, during all of his resurrection-life. He spent his time in showing how his own life was an unfoldment of the Old Testament Scriptures. He rebuked them and all others who fail to see him in the Old Testament, in the words, "O fools, and slow of heart to believe all that the prophets have spoken! Ought not Christ to have suffered these things, and to enter into his glory? And beginning at Moses, and all the prophets, he expounded to them in all the Scriptures the things concerning himself." He showed them the truth of his own words, "that all things must be fulfilled, which were written in the law of Moses, and in the prophets, and in the Psalms, concerning me." Is Christ to be believed? If not, then it is useless to study his words or to attach importance to either Testament. But if he is to be believed, then these prophets, beginning with Moses, and all these Scriptures enfolded great truths concerning him, which were literally unfolded in his divine-human history. To search these Scriptures and to find in them nothing of Christ, nothing of how he was to suffer, to die, and to enter into his glory, is to understand them in a vastly different manner from that taught by our divine Lord. On this journey, without doubt, he referred to some of the great leading prophecies concerning himself.

His hearers were familiar with these special portions of the Old Testament. We can well believe that he began with the promise given at Eden's gate regarding the seed of the woman; that he moved forward to the covenant with Abraham, to the Paschal Lamb, to the exodus from Egypt, to the raising up of the prophet like unto himself; to the Shechinah, the tabernacle, the mercy-seat, the manna, and the brazen serpent; to the vision of Isaiah, when he saw his glory, to the prophecy of Daniel that the Messiah should come, and to other similar Scriptures.

Wonderful exposition—glorious expositor—happy hearers! No wonder that their hearts burned within them as he opened to them the Scriptures. That very morning he had burst the barriers of the grave; that day angels honored the place where his head and feet had lain. He was the incarnate God, fresh from his victory on the cross and over the grave, and going forward to his place on the throne; and yet he spent more time that afternoon speaking to an audience of two, doing the word of a Sunday-school teacher, expounding the Old Testament Scriptures, showing how they are unfolded in his own life, than he ever spent, so far as the record informs us, in instructing any other hearers during his resurrection-life. Dr. Pentecost, in his instructive little book entitled " In the Volume of the Book," tells us that "there are nearly one thousand direct quotations from or allusions to the Old Testament Scriptures in the New, and that every book in the Old Testament, unless it be the Book of Esther, is quoted from or alluded to in the lines of the New Testament." In the words of John the Baptist, "Behold the Lamb of God that taketh away the sin of the world," we have unfolded all the Old Testament references to the Paschal Lamb and the blood sprinkled on the door-posts on that dreadful night in Egypt. We are also reminded that the Messiah was to be brought as a lamb to the slaughter, and also of the lamb sacrificed on Jewish altars through the long series of symbolic years. In his words to Nicodemus, "As Moses lifted up the serpent in the wilderness, even so must the Son of Man be lifted up," we have unfolded the wonderful story of the brazen serpent in the twenty-first chapter of the Book of Numbers. In the reference to our being "made nigh by the blood of Christ," Eph. ii. 13, we have unfolded the Old Testament reference to the law of sacrifice and to the divisions of the Temple. The Epistle to the Romans unfolds to us the Book of Genesis, and the Epistle to the Hebrews the Book of Leviticus. The New Testament is the developed truths which were in germ in the Old. Every part of the revelation is perfect in its place. The rivulet is perfect as a rivulet, the river as a river. Jesus, we are told, increased in wisdom and in stature, and in favor with God and man. But he was perfect as a boy as truly as he was perfect as a man. The idea of growth in the Word of God is no reflection upon its perfection. Each part is perfect in its time and place. Neither is the human element in the Word of God any reflection upon its perfection. The incarnate Word was human as well as divine, and his humanity is an imperishable element in the glory of his divinity. He was divinity humanized, and in the humanization of the divine we have in some degree the divinization of the human.

The revealed Word is also human and divine, and as truly may we say of it as of him that the human element adds to the glory of the divine element. A revelation for the human race must come through human forms of speech. The reader of the Old Testament must feel, as Robinson expressed himself to the Pilgrim Fathers when leaving England, " I am very confident the Lord hath more truth yet to break forth out of his holy Word." Standing in the light of the New Testament he discovers that more truth has broken forth, and that its beneficent rays are falling upon his upturned face and rejoicing his grateful heart.

We have also in the teaching of the apostles similar unfoldments of the Old Testament narratives. We have often felt that we would give much to have heard Christ expounding Moses and the prophets and the Psalms concerning himself. Without doubt he spent a considerable part of the forty days in doing this work; and without doubt the apostles in the early days of the Church, when the spirit came upon them in mighty power, were imitating his example. We have in their teachings, we may be sure, the substance of our Lord's expositions. The epistles are the echoes of those wonderful conversations with the disciples. The early sermons of the disciples unfold the teachings of the Lord under the guidance of the Spirit. Few studies could be more profitable than a careful analysis of the sermons of the apostles. On the day of Pentecost the apostle Peter showed how the Old Testament unfolded the truths concerning Christ, and his sermon shows us how we may unfold in our sermons and Sunday-school lessons these same truths to indifferent hearers or to anxious inquirers. Stephen followed the example of Peter and of the Master. His sermon is cogent in reasoning, eloquent in appeal, and mighty in Scripture throughout. How gloriously Philip made known to the Ethiopian treasurer the things concerning the Lord. He unfolds that blessed chapter of Isaiah so that our hearts rejoice as we follow the earnest evangelist and his interesting inquirer. The Acts of the Apostles has been called the Gospel of the Risen Jesus, or the Gospel of the Holy Ghost. It tells the same story as the gospels; it unfolds the same precious truths regarding Old Testament prophecy. Gloriously does the matchless Paul unfold the Old Testament story in sermon and in epistle, in prayer, and in doxology.

The Bible has been and is in the fierce fires of modern criticism. Some of the scaffolds men have built in creed and in confession, in interpretation and exposition, around the temple of truth may be rudely torn down. Let them go. They have often deformed the glorious Temple of God. Let the Bible be true, though all creeds be false. Thank God, it is read, understood, believed, loved, and lived now as never before in the history of the Church; thank God, it will stand through all the ages. "The grass" of infidel oratory, and sometimes of so-called Christian teaching, "withereth, and the flower" of sceptical reasoning and creedal teaching "falleth, but the Word of the Lord abideth forever." Let each pray, with the loving George Herbert:

> "Oh, that I knew how all thy lights combine,
>   And the configuration of their glory!
> Seeing not only how each verse doth shine,
>   But all the constellations of the story!"

XII.

No More Sea.

"*And there was no more sea.*"—REV. xxi. 1.

THE 21st chapter of Revelations describes the triumphant state of the redeemed Church with all its conflicts over and all its enemies destroyed. That happy condition is represented under the image of a beautiful city, the New Jerusalem which John in vision saw descending out of heaven. Jerusalem was to the Hebrew the symbol of the heavenly world; the peculiar dwelling-place of God. But this New Jerusalem has no temple, for it is all temple; it has no light, for it is all light. "The Lord God Almighty and the Lamb are the temple of it," "and the Lamb is the light thereof." But nothing struck John more forcibly than that in it "there was no more sea." This places heaven in marked contrast with the earth. Here three-fourths of the surface of the globe are occupied with seas and oceans; and thus these parts of the earth are unfit for the dwelling-place of men. Perhaps one thought in the mind of the apostle was, that in heaven there would be no wastes of water; that all parts of this redeemed earth would be habitable.

But his meaning is deeper. Figurative as the language is, there is deep significance in the figure. All nature is voiceful, if only we be attentive to her teaching. We go far to see a painting which is the work of man's hand, if only it shows the touch of genius. Thousands yearly make pilgrimages to Dresden to stand in admiration, akin to adoration, before Raphael's matchless Madonna, and they do well. But we are often strangely insensible to the pictures which God lays on the bosom of mother earth, or hangs in peerless splendor on the arch of the heavens. God is the greatest of painters. Earth and air, sea and sky declare his power, his •wisdom and his love. "In his hand are the deep places of the earth; the strength of the hills is his also. The sea is his, and he made it; and his hands formed the dry land."

This truth led the psalmist immediately to cry out: "Oh come, let us worship and bow down; let us kneel before the Lord our Maker." In heaven the absence of the sea is cause for praise. Why is this? What is the meaning of this figurative language? This is an interesting question, and to it a definite answer can be given.

I. The sea, in the conception of the ancient He-

brews, stood for separation between individuals and
nations; but in heaven there will be no such separation. The Hebrews were not a seafaring people.
David had a varied experience as a shepherd, a
soldier, an outlaw, a courtier, a poet and a king; but
he was never a sailor. With all his wonderful ad-
ventures, he seems never to have had a personal experience of either the delights or the dangers of the
sea. Solomon with all his means of pleasure does
not seem ever to have owned a yacht. The man in
those early days who had been to Ophir or Tarshish
would be a hero on his return. Men, women and
children would sit at his feet to hear the story of his
wonderful exploits.

Still, beautiful allusions to the sea are found in the
writings of Hebrew prophets and poets. From the
mountains of Palestine they could look down on the
changeful Mediterranean in her different moods.
They often watched the tempest ploughing the sea
into foam, and dashing it in fury on the rocky face
of Carmel; and thus it came to pass that often the
divine message of the sacred writers was delivered
in the sublime imagery of the deep. To express the
idea of great sorrow the psalmist speaks of deep calling unto deep, wave following wave, and billows
going over his soul.

Christ's dominion is represented as extending from
sea to sea, and the glory of heaven is as the sound of

many waters. No writers have better described the
majesty of the sea when " the stormy wind which lift-
eth up the waves thereof." This is especially illustrated in the 107th Psalm. All commentators are
agreed that this is the most highly finished and
thoroughly poetic of all the pictures of human deliverance. It is, as Perowne suggests, a landsman's
picture; but yet that of one who knew much of the
dangers of the deep. We have the waves running mountains high; then the weakness of human skill, then the joy of the calm, and finally
the desired haven. The same author quotes Ad-
dison in the *Spectator* as saying that he prefers
this description of a ship in a storm before any
other he has met with; and he adds: " How much
more comfortable as well as rational, is this system
of the psalmist than the Pagan scheme in Virgil and
other poets, where one deity is represented as raising
a storm and another as laying it! Were we only to
consider the sublime in this piece of poetry, what
can be nobler than the idea it gives us of the Supreme Being thus raising a tumult among the elements, and recovering them out of their confusion;
thus troubling and becalming nature?"

To-day the sea is not thought of as a line of separation; for now it is the highway of nations. Now on
its surface go the great ships; and far down on its
bed lies the cable which makes " the world a whis-

pering gallery." But still on earth separations exist.
Duty often places us on the earth at great distances
from our friends; and there is a sea lying between
time and eternity which our friends cannot cross to
come to us, nor we, when in life, to go to them.
Although we listen ever so intently we cannot hear
their voices; although we wait ever so patiently we
cannot see their forms. A cold, dark sea rolls between us and them. There is no cable at its bottom;
there is no ship on its surface. Thank God, the day
is coming when there shall be no more sea. When
the angel shall stand upon the sea and upon the
earth and shall say that there shall be time no
longer; then the sea also shall be no more.

There are separations in the social world. Great
chasms exist in society. Caste distinctions unfortunately exist. The spirit of the world divides society
horizontally, each layer being allied to its kindred
layer in the social scale. The Spirit of Christ divides
society vertically; it cuts through all the layers. It
recognizes every man's manhood; it estimates men
not according to what they have, but according to
what they are. Men of the world have talked much
of "Liberty, Equality and Fraternity." These have
been catch-words of bloody revolutions. They have
been alike the inspiration of noble endeavors and of
satanic ambitions. But the sea still flows on, now
calmly, now wildly, between different classes in

social life. The Church of Christ is the true leveller of social conditions; it levels society by lifting the down-trodden; it levels upward. When the Spirit of Christ prevails the spirit of true Liberty, Equality and Fraternity will prevail. With all its faults, the Russian Church sets a good example in that in its public worship all classes are on a level before God. Princes and peasants bow together at the same altar. This Church of ours stands for this Christian idea. Here there is in this sense no sea; here there are no class distinctions. The rich and the poor meet together and learn that the Lord is the Maker of them all. When Christ is fully recognized on earth there shall be no more sea between the various classes on earth; and in heaven, in the largest sense, in this respect there is no more sea.

There are also on earth separations in the intellectual world. Some men live apart from their fellows in lofty philosophical speculations; they live in an ideal world. They are in advance of their age; they wander in solitariness among the mountain peaks of thought. Great superiority must always pay the penalty of loneliness; these men others will leave severely alone, or reluctantly follow, or violently oppose. The heart of such thinkers is lonely within them; a sea flows about them. But the day is coming for them, if they be pure in heart as they are clear in thought, when there shall be no sea.

The day is coming when all earnest students of truth shall be enthroned as kings in truth's vast and glorious realm. Between many Christians there now flows a sea. Differing denominational views separate them; different degrees of attainment in the divine life are also barriers. Some grovel; others soar. Some live in the valleys; others on the mountain top. Some in the porter's lodge; others in the king's palace. Some live among transfiguration splendors; others only in the deep shadows of Gethsemane. Days of harmony, of development, and of exaltation are coming. Drawing nearer to Christ all true disciples will draw nearer to one another, and even on the earth they shall have foretastes of the harmony of heaven.

II. The sea stands for mystery; in heaven mysteries will largely pass away. The sea is mysterious in its volume and its movements. Three-quarters of the surface of the globe are covered with it. The psalmist is right when he speaks of "the abundance of the sea;" the poets are wrong who speak of "the wild waste of waters," and of the "barren, barren sea." It is not barren; it is not a lawless mass of surging waters. It is subject still to the voice of God. The sea prevents the earth from becoming a waste. It furnishes water for thirsty souls, and for the parched grasses, plants, and trees; its warm currents make great tracts, which otherwise would be utterly unfit for man, habitable and fruitful.

Think of the balancing of forces which keeps the ocean in its bed while the world spins upon its axis forty times faster than flies the swiftest train. The moon as she moves through the heavens controls the tidal waves of the deep. Let any of these great movements be disarranged and the sea would rush upon the land and all human life would be destroyed.

Creation is a mystery. Life in its origin is a problem which godless biologists can never solve. The ways of Providence are past finding out in our present state of ignorance. Redemption is a sublime mystery of love and grace. Now we see through a glass darkly: hereafter eye to eye. Now we know in part: hereafter even as we are known. Now we know Christ as we are: hereafter we shall know him as he is. Now we see Christ in his word and works: hereafter we shall see him face to face. Then in that beatific vision we shall know him as we are known. All hail the day when mysteries shall disappear and when the glory of the knowledge of God and his works shall flood our souls and rejoice our hearts!

III. The sea stands for danger; in heaven there shall be no more sea. Perhaps, to the ancient Hebrews, the sea was a symbol of destructive power more than anything else. It is indeed a fearful monster; it is terrible in its wrath, and awful in its majesty. It charms and terrifies; it smiles in joy and frowns in anger. It allures like a mother; it destroys like a demon. Some of the ancients compared it to a great animal, its tides being its breathing-times. The comparison is appropriate; the sea opens its mouth and swallows its victims; then it smiles and looks innocent as a child. It is cunning, deceptive, terrible. Its waves, as they break in the evening along the shores, seem like huge serpents gleaming and hissing. It has its moods; sailors understand them and guard against each fickle change. The ancients were comparatively helpless; they were without steam, without compass, without skill. No wonder the apostle Paul and his companions "were driven up and down in Adria." The sea broke the ships and destroyed the lives of the early Hebrew mariners; they reeled to and fro, they staggered like drunken men, they were at their wit's end. They saw the wonders of the Lord in the deep; and they trembled at his great power.

And with all our boasted progress, the sea is still often our master. Within recent years, many great ships have gone to the bottom. We are humiliated in the presence of these great disasters. Four o'clock in the morning has been lately the fatal hour for great ships. At that hour the majestic "Oregon" received the fatal blow; at that hour, a few weeks ago, the "Thingvalla" and the "Geiser," sister ships, ran into each other; at that hour the watches are changed and the men are not fully awake to danger and duty. As

12

a result, the Cunard Line has recently changed its watches, so as to give all the officers longer hours of continuous sleep during the twenty-four. Life stands for danger. Physical dangers abound; they make existence a constant struggle. With the dangers from false faiths, we are sadly familiar. As men believe, so are they. Moral shipwrecks lie along life's course. But the day is coming when the sea of danger will utterly disappear. We remember that at the funeral of an eloquent preacher of the gospel, his widow was surprisingly calm and even happy. To an inquirer as to the cause of her composure, she said: "Thank God, he is safe now; temptation can never reach him again." He had fallen under the power of the intoxicating cup. He repented of his sin, and was restored to his place in the church of God; but he trembled constantly on the edge of the precipice. Now he had gone upward; the danger was over, and his wife was joyous in the thought that temptation would never again reach him. Once there trod the waves of the Galilean Sea their Lord and Master. He who trod the waters of that sea and bade its boisterous waves "be still," still rules the stormy sea of life. "O Lord God of Hosts, who is like unto thee? Thou rulest the raging of the sea; when the waves thereof arise, thou stillest them."

There is a Pilot who can bear us safely over the

sea to the haven of that land where the sea itself
shall be no more.   Let us then in simple faith utter
this prayer:

> "Jesus, Saviour, pilot me
>   Over life's tempestuous sea;
> Unknown waves before me roll,
>   Hiding rock and treacherous shoal;
> Chart and compass came from thee;
>   Jesus, Saviour, pilot me."

XIII.

The Christian's Certain Comfort.

W E have just crossed the boundary line between
the old year and the new. We would be more
or less than human did not solemn thoughts fill our
minds to-day. Longfellow, in his "Evangeline,"
speaks of the strange fears of coming ill which at
times we all feel, and adds:

"As, at the tramp of a horse's hoof on the turf of the prairies,
Far in advance are closed the leaves of the shrinking mi-
mosa,
So, at the hoof-beats of fate, with sad forebodings of evil,
Shrinks and closes the heart, ere the stroke of doom has at-
tained it."

Perhaps our hearts tremble as we begin the new
year and listen for the hoof-beats of God's possible
providences before the year shall close. What messengers shall come? Shall some dark shadow fall over
home or heart? Who can tell? Thank God, no one
can tell. We go out into the opening year trusting
in his divine care and almighty love.

It has been for some time our custom to give on the
first Sunday morning of the new year a passage of

Scripture which may serve as a motto-text for the year. It is known that these new-year texts, because of the emphasis which the occasion gives them, have been a *vade mecum* to many; and that they have made joy more joyous, and sorrow less grievous. Some of our number who are absent from us send for them regularly, and are much helped by them during the year; and some have them, as the result of various artistic devices, always before their eyes in their homes. Their selection has come, therefore, to be a matter of careful thought and earnest prayer. The passage chosen for this year is this:

" . . . *Surely I know that it shall be well with them that fear God, which fear before him.*"—ECCLES. viii. 12.

In the former part of this verse the character and condition of sinners are contrasted with those of the righteous. However long the sinner lives in sin, and however prosperous he may seem to be, yet it shall be ill with him; but however it may seem sometimes to be with the righteous man, in the long run it shall be well with him. It will readily be admitted by all that Solomon was a competent witness. He had tasted the so-called sweetness of sin in all its forms; he had partaken of its various cups even to satiety. Repeatedly has he given us the deliberate results of his wide and varied experiences. His words ought to have great weight. This text is well calculated to check the folly and presumption of the sinner, and to comfort the righteous man in the trials of life; and especially in the apparent delay of justice in permitting the triumphs of the ungodly.

THE PERSONS DESCRIBED.

Notice, in the first place, the persons who are here described—"them that fear God." This is in the Word of God a common designation of the people of God. The fear of the Lord is emphasized as the beginning of wisdom. What is meant by this fear? What kind of fear is it? It is certainly not servile fear. It may have something of that character in its beginning; but it does not long continue in that atmosphere. Experience proves that many a Christian begins his Christian life with the fear of God in its lowest sense, the fear of punishment, as its inspiring motive. Better that than a life of indifference to truth and God. The Bible does appeal to that element; we are taught to fear him who can destroy both soul and body in hell. The heart has many doors; over one is written Faith, over another Hope, over another Love. The Word of God knocks at each of these doors. In the case of one man the heart is entered by one door; in the case of another man by another door. The man who is learning a new language, or learning to speak his own correctly, speaks for a time laboriously under the fear of violating some grammatical rule; but after a time the knowledge of the language becomes a part of his very nature, and he rises above the fear of violating the rules of grammar and comes into the love of correct speech. So, starting in the Christian life on the low plane of fear in its lower senses, we may rise into the perfect love of God which casteth out all fear; we learn to love truth, to love holiness and to love God for their own sake; we would serve God if there were no hell to be shunned, and no heaven to be won; and we come finally to think little of either as motives in life and work, for then the love of Christ constraineth us. At this stage in our Christian lives we fear simply lest we may offend God, our Father, Friend, and Redeemer.

This latter fear is truly filial; it is the fear of a son and not that of a slave. Christians are the sons and daughters of the Lord Almighty. They have received the adoption of sons; they cry, Abba, Father. Theirs is a holy, humble, fiducial fear; it is a loving confidence; it is an affectionate trust. When a man is adopted into God's family and is living in full and blessed consciousness of that adoption, he will serve God because of the joy of that service. He is then a new man; he is influenced by new motives; he is under the control of the constraining love of Christ. It is a false pride which leads a man to call himself a slave when God calls him a son. The Prodigal

Son expected to say on his return: "Father, I have sinned against heaven, and before Thee, and am no more worthy to be called thy son; make me as one of thy hired servants;" but when his father's kiss was on his cheek and the sense of forgiving love in his heart, all the words which he had conned over were not uttered. He says, indeed: "Father, I have sinned against heaven, and in thy sight, and am no more worthy to be called thy son," but there he stops. The Father's voice is instantly heard saying: "Bring forth the best robe, and put it on him." Filial love is now filling his soul. When Louis the Fourteenth would test the courtesy of Lord Chesterfield—or, according to some authorities, the Earl of Stair—he had his carriage door opened and asked the nobleman to step in first, and he immediately stepped in, leaving the king to follow. Louis complimented him for having maintained his reputation for gentlemanliness, and his reply was, "I hope I am too much of a gentleman to refuse the request of a king." We ought to be too humble to refuse the request of the King of Heaven. True humility takes the place which God gives; to refuse is not humility but culpable unbelief.

It is genuine, sincere, honest, and hearty fear which God's people possess. This characteristic of their fear is taught us by the latter part of the verse which says, "which fear before him." This description suggests the transparent, the godly fear which is here commended. It is far removed from the fear of the hypocrite. This true fear comes from the bottom of the soul. It is genuine even in the presence of the omnipresent and omniscient God. This is the only religion which endures the test; it will bear the scrutiny of men and angels, of time and eternity, and will receive at last the approval of God.

THE PROMISE HERE GIVEN.

Observe, in the second place, the promise concerning the people of God: "It shall be well with them." This is a modest and, we may say, inadequate putting of this great certainty. Much more is implied than is expressed. Often this is the strongest way of stating a great truth; conscious of its greatness the speaker designedly expresses it only partially. Neither saint nor seraph can tell all that is included in this "well." Ask Enoch; ask Paul. What shall they answer? Only this: "Eye hath not seen, nor ear heard, neither have entered into the heart of man, the things which God hath prepared for them that love him."

It is not said that believers shall not have their share in the ordinary trials of life. The Bible nowhere promises us exemption from these trials. It does not assure us that we shall not go into the furnace, nor into the deep waters; but it does promise that the fire shall not consume us and the waters shall not overflow us. In the midst of the trial it shall still be well with us. By our side in the furnace there shall be One who is like the Son of God, and we shall come out without even the smell of fire on our garments. It is not said that Christians shall not have extraordinary trials. Christianity develops manhood; it vastly enlarges the sphere of life. It gives a broader surface across which the winds of adversity may sweep. It gives greater possibilities of enjoyment; and these make greater trials certain. A Christian man is higher, and deeper, and broader than other men are. He is more fully developed in all his capacities both for joy and sorrow. Christ suffered unspeakably more than any other man who ever lived could suffer. He had in himself all the nobleness of man and all the gentleness of woman; he had vaster capacities of suffering than other men possess. Stoical indifference to pain is an evidence of a coarse and brutal nature. To feel, and yet to do and dare, is to be truly noble. Intellectual attainment and spiritual culture increase the number and exquisiteness of our faculties and capacities. The more our natures are developed the greater also will be our responsibilities. Loyalty to God put Joseph into prison; made Elijah face cruel Ahab and wicked Jezebel; drove Daniel into a den of lions; hurled the three faithful Hebrews into the seven times heated furnace; put Peter into the common prison and Paul and Silas into the inner prison and made their feet fast in the stocks. But it was still well with them. This fact is the glory of our faith; this is the joy of our life in God. Joseph finds his prison the vestibule to the palace of the Pharaohs; Elijah's fiery mission is but the prelude to the chariot of fire and glorious translation. From Bunyan's prison goes forth his Pilgrim to carry his name and his Lord's to the ends of the earth; from Luther's castle prison goes forth the German Bible, the bulwark of the German throne and nation, and of Protestantism throughout the world. It is not said that believers shall not often be in an evil case. This condition is inevitable. They shall at times seem to be utterly overthrown; but they shall still triumph in God. Quaintly has it been said that all "God's people are like birds: they sing best in cages." Out of their deepest sorrows come their sweetest songs; when most bruised they send forth the most fragrant odors. From her bed of excruciating pain Anne Steele sent out her hymns of faith, hope, and love. But for her sorrow the Church had not been cheered by her "Father! whate'er of earthly bliss." God's people know that all things work together for good to those who love him. They know that no form of trial, that neither death nor life shall be able to separate them from the love of God which is in

Christ Jesus their Lord.   Looking up to God in
deepest grief they can say:

> "If from thy ordeal's heated bars
> Our feet are seamed with crimson scars,
> Thy will be done!"

ASSURED KNOWLEDGE EXPRESSED.

Notice, in the third place, the absolute certainty
here expressed: "Yet surely I know." There is
power in absolute certainty. There are those who
magnify and multiply their doubts.   To doubt, they
think, is an evidence of unusual intellectual acumen;
it is rather a proof of mental feebleness.   Doubt is
the gray dawn of the morning; faith is the splendor
of the noonday sun.   Doubt is childhood; faith is
manhood, manhood in its prime and glory.   Paul
rang out his "I know."   The blind man who had
been cured triumphantly said, "I know."   The
Apostle John confidently repeats, "We know."   To-
day, there are disciples of certain schools who can
only say, "perhaps," "possibly," "peradventure."
These men are agnostics; that is, know-nothings.
No man ought to preach his doubts; audiences have
doubts enough of their own.   If some of us were to
preach all that we do not know we would have an
endless theme.   If we have doubts, let us tell them
to God; if we have truths, let us tell them to men.
Thank God for men and women who are know-some-

things! In the midst of earthly loss and pain they can say, "We know it shall be well."

The inspired preacher had good grounds for his knowledge. Because of God's character men may be sure that it will be well with those who fear him. God must be right; God must do right. One wrong on God's part and he would no longer be God. One wrong act would overturn his throne; a God who can sin is no God. If God could sin there would be a world without a God, and a kingdom without a throne. His highest claim to our homage is his infinite rightness. Mere power on God's part could not compel homage on our part. God, by his power, might crush me, but cannot compel my love; but when he shows me a Father's love, how can I, except I be an utter ingrate, withhold from him a son's gratitude? "Worship God," said the angel to the overawed Apostle John. Why? The completest answer is, because God is infinitely the best Being in the universe. If you can find a better being than God, worship that other being. The history of God's people emphasizes also the truth that it is well with them that fear God. The experience of each believer proves it for himself. Do you fear God? If not, begin to-day. If you do fear him, rest sweetly on his great and precious promise.

Let us, like Enoch, walk with God through the months and days of this new year. And to walk

with God we must go in the same direction; two
cannot walk together except they be agreed.   Enoch
walked and walked with God till they reached the
limits of time and earth; and still kept on walking
with him; walked into eternity, into heaven; walks
with him still.   Some who begin the year with us
will end it with God.   God alone knows what of
trial this year has in store for each of us.   But above
all the sounds of life's trials shall be our note of
triumph in God who will bring us off more than
conquerors; and in eternity the sweetest strain of
our immortal song shall be, "He hath done all things
well."

XIV.

Seeking and Receiving.

"But seek ye first the kingdom of God, and his righteous-ness; and all these things shall be added unto you."—MATT. vi. 33.

THIS text is a part of the Sermon on the Mount. That sermon is one of the most solemn and instructive portions of the Bible. It lifts Jesus Christ above all other teachers of the world; it alone furnishes a strong argument for his divinity. If we deny his divinity it will be impossible to explain his wisdom as a teacher as seen in this wonderful discourse. The Christ of the Cross does not appear very conspicuously here; but the Christ of the Throne here reigns gloriously. He lays down the laws of his new kingdom; he places before us the exalted standard of ideal perfection which that kingdom demands. This discourse is, as I understand it, an exhortation unto repentance. It is, in this respect, like the instruction which Christ gave the lawyer who stood up tempting him and asking: "What

shall I do to inherit eternal life?" Before him Jesus
lifted the standard of the ideal life and character.
The design of the sermon is to lead all men to cry
out with the disciples when in the storm on the
Galilean Sea: "Lord, save us: we perish!" Every
honest man who reads this discourse must feel that
without divine help he can never attain to the perfection of conduct and character here enjoined. Men
often say that they do not want the doctrinal religion
often preached in our pulpits and enforced in many
parts of the Bible; that they want only the religion
of the Sermon on the Mount. It must be said that
these men do not know whereof they speak. The
Sermon on the Mount does not lower the standard
of life and duty—it exalts it. The thoughtful moral-
ist who said, "God save me at the day of judgment
from the Sermon on the Mount," better understood
its high, broad, and deep spiritual teaching. This
sermon is really designed to lead every reader to say,
with the publican, "God be merciful to me a sinner."

1. In studying this text let us notice, in the first
place, what we are to seek—"the kingdom of God
and his righteousness." In previous verses Christ
prohibited in various ways the undue seeking after
the things of the world. He earnestly rebukes all
undue solicitude about the things of this life. But
thus far his instructions on this point have been
negative; now, however, he advances a step. These

world objects are not to be avoided by a mere nega-
tion; by simply attempting to abstain from unnecessary anxiety and unbelief no one will be likely to
succeed. The best way to correct the evil here rebuked is to seek to do the good here suggested. The
best way to get rid of undue care about unnecessary
things is to have a due care about necessary things.
The best way to drive out darkness is to let in the
light; the best way to keep evil out of the heart is to
fill it with good. Right seeking is the true remedy
against false seeking. Christ was a wise teacher.
He recognized the fundamental laws of moral and
mental action. He needed not that any one should
tell him, for he knew what was in man. This is
the principle which Dr. Chalmers emphasized when
he talked of "the expulsive power of a new affection." If we subordinate the affairs of this life to
the concerns of the other life, both lives will be
brought into their proper relations, and both then
will be taken at their true value. It will also be
observed that the subordination of this life to the
other does not exclude a proper consideration of the
affairs of this life; on the contrary, it includes and
emphasizes their right consideration and secures their
fullest performance. Such subordination is true wisdom; its absence brings chaos and ends in eternal loss.

We understand by "the kingdom of God and his
righteousness" the seeking and observing of the prin-
13

ciples of that kingdom which Christ was about to set
up. Righteousness here is not to be taken in the
technical and theological sense of the imputed righteousness of Christ—at least, not primarily; it is,
rather, seeking to do God's will, to observe what he
esteems right, what he has made right, what is
right. It is a constant subjection of our will to
God's; a performance of right things in a right
spirit. Seeking in this way to promote God's kingdom would at the same time most effectually promote
our true interests, spiritual and eternal, temporal
and secular. So far as the disciples were concerned
Christ would say: "You are pupils in my school;
continue to live for me; make my will the law of
your life." So far as others in his audience were
concerned, Christ here says: "Enter on my service;
enlist under my banner; this is the great concern;
this is the one thing needful; seek the purity of
heart and the holiness of life which God requires and
which you must possess in order to become the subjects of my kingdom." In a word, by the kingdom
of God and his righteousness, I understand Christ
to say to us, "Accept salvation through me, submit
to my claims; give me the homage of your hearts."
This is the demand which Christ makes of us to-day
in this Scripture.

2. Notice that this great good is *to be sought*—
"seek ye first," etc. The word translated seek is a

strong one; it means seek earnestly, intensely, again and again; it includes the idea of eagerness, solicitude, importunity. So elsewhere Christ tells us to strive, to agonize, as did the wrestler or the racer, to enter in at the strait gate. The gate is strait, and so difficult to enter; the way is narrow, and so difficult to continue therein. To be lost needs no searching for the way, for all are in it already. To go with the current is easy; to oppose it is difficult. Men who float with the tide have no proper conception of its force. A dead fish can float, but it takes a live one to go up stream.

This law of seeking in order to finding is in harmony with the rule of life in every department of effort. If a man wants money, he must seek it; if he wants learning, he must pay its price in hard study. Ignorance he may have without effort. To raise thistles, a man need not prepare the ground nor sow the seed; to raise wheat, he must do both. Toil is evermore the standard of value. Cost and worth are ever close neighbors. Only by the rugged path of toil do men reach the heights of great attainment; only by paying the price of heroic effort do they write their names high in the temple of fame. We are all familiar with the answer of Euclid to King Ptolemy Lagus when he asked, " Is there not a shorter and easier way to the study of geometry than that which you have laid down in your Elements?" His

reply was, "There is no royal road to geometry."
There is no road to heaven but that of sacrifice,
that of cross-bearing; we must go in this narrow
way or not at all.   But it is also a way of joy, a path
of pleasantness and peace.   You must not expect to
become a Christian by accident.   That blessed experience must be the result of deliberate determina-
tion, of intelligent seeking, and of faithful enduring.
This truth is earnestly affirmed in many parts of
Christ's teaching.   Christ's honesty is worthy of
commendation.   He clearly lays down the conditions
of discipleship; we must take up the cross and follow
him.

3.   We next learn in the text the order of our seeking: "Seek ye *first* the kingdom of God and his
righteousness."   Here is declared the right order in
which our seeking of earthly and heavenly things is
to take place.   The care of the soul is to take prece-
dence of all other care; and the affairs of this life are
thus to be made secondary to those of the life to
come.   Just here many make their fatal mistake.
They give earthly things the first place in their
thought; they set God and his claims aside entirely,
or give them a subordinate place.   They desire the
advantages of religion, but they are unwilling to
perform its duties.   Like the rich young man, they
wish to inherit eternal life, but they are not willing
to take up their cross and follow their Lord.   When

the claims of religion are pressed upon them like
Felix, they say: "Go thy way for this time." Now
if religion be not worth everything it is worth
nothing. Look the matter squarely in the face;
decide it like honorable and sensible men. If God's
claims are just, they are supreme. Give him the
first place in your heart. Dethrone every idol;
enthrone the Lord Jesus. Let us stop shilly-shally-
ing. Let us not be like the heathen colonists whom
"the king of Assyria brought from Babylon, and
from Cuthah, and from Avah, and from Hamath,"
and placed in the cities of Samaria instead of the
children of Israel. It is said of them, "They feared
the Lord and served their own gods." This description is unfortunately true of too many who call themselves Christians. Oh, for a holy enthusiasm in
Christ's cause! Tradition says that the artist Correggio, when young, saw with rapturous joy a painting by Raphael—it is said to have been St. Cecilia at
Bologna—upon which he gazed in transports of
delight. His soul drank in its beauty as flowers
drink moisture from the dew. Artistic genius was
enkindled within him; the blood rushed to his brow
and fire flashed from his eyes as he cried out: "I,
too, am a painter!" That conviction upheld him in
his dark hours; it blended with his colors; it guided
his pencil; it glowed on his canvas. His art was
first in his thought and attainment. Success crowned

his untiring zeal and his heroic toils.   Titian, on wit-
nessing his production, exclaimed: "Were I not
Titian, I would wish to be Correggio." The word
enthusiasm comes from a Greek word which means
to be inspired or possessed of God.   If Christ be in
the soul a holy enthusiasm must mark our lives.   If
the love of Christ constrain us, we cannot but speak
of what we have seen and felt of that mighty love.
Away with lukewarmness!   A half-way Christian
is an object of contempt to devils and of pity to
angels!   Let us put God first.   Around him let the
affairs of this life revolve as do planets about the
sun.   Other things are to be sought in their proper
time and place, but God first.   He cannot, he will
not share his glory with any.   The first commandment thunders in our ears, "Thou shalt have no
other gods before me."   We may have other objects
of love, but not *before* God; if we do, we are idola-
ters.   The man who puts this world first is like the
man who gathers pebbles while pearls lie unnoticed
at his feet.   Money, learning, position, power—these
are right, these are to be sought.   But each in its
own order.   We are to seek God first in time.   Let
youth be consecrated to his service; let its first love
be his; let it in its sweetness and freshness be laid
on his altar.   Seek God first in affection.   I say, be
a Christian to-day in every drop of your blood, in
every thought of your heart, and in every act of

life. Despise yourself that you have so long been double-minded and unstable. Break with the world; cleave unto God. To every temptation of sin and Satan give a ringing NO! Those are stirring words of Lord Macaulay, uttered during the agitation of a turbulent political contest at Leeds. He was anxious, of course, to secure the votes of the electors, but he would not stoop to play a double part. To the electors he plainly declared his opinions, but he would give no pledges. He thought it as improper that an Englishman should be courted and fawned upon in his capacity of elector as in his capacity of juryman. Much as he might want their votes, he far more highly valued their esteem; and he concludes with this sentence: "It is not necessary to my happiness that I should sit in Parliament, but it is necessary to my happiness that I should possess, in Parliament or out of Parliament, the consciousness of having done what is right."

4. Notice the reward which Christ gives to those who seek aright: "And all these things shall be added unto you." By seeking God first you shall have the kingdom, and over and above you shall have all other necessary things. A great problem confronts every man: How shall I win both worlds? Christ here gives us the solution: Seek first the kingdom of God. Having done that, over and above, you shall have food and raiment. Great wealth is

not promised, but necessary things are. If a man seeks God, he can then cast all his care on him, leaving the bestowment or denial of worldly things to the allotment of his wisdom and love. An old writer, in illustrating this thought, says: "He who buys goods has paper and pack-thread given him into the bargain." Solomon asked for wisdom, and God, pleased with his choice, said: "And I have also given thee that which thou hast not asked, both riches and honor; so that there shall not be any among the kings like unto thee all thy days." Paul, in writing to Timothy, says: "Godliness is profitable unto all things, having promise of the life that now is, and of that which is to come." What a blessed change would be wrought in the world if this truth were grounded in our hearts and illustrated in our lives! It was a common saying among the Jews, "Seek that to which other things are added;" and this truth was illustrated in this way: A king said to his particular friend, "Ask what thou wilt and I shall give it thee." He thought within himself, if I ask to be made a general I shall get my request; but I will ask something to which many and better things are added. He therefore said, "Give me thy daughter to wife." This he did knowing that all the dignities of the kingdom would be added to his request.

This was a wise man. The man who thinks to

serve God and mammon must fail utterly. It is impossible to unite these two forms of service. God first; this is Christ's law. God's kingdom stands. They who live for Christ live for the eternities. Their life takes hold of that within the veil. Not one jot or one tittle of Christ's promise shall fail. The mount on which he stood when he uttered his immortal discourse we know not; the audience that listened is gone; kingdoms have risen and fallen, but Christ's words stand. It is eternally true that they that seek God first shall have the mastery over both worlds.

Prepare in the heart, in the home, and in the entire life the first place for royal majesty. Make room to-day for Jesus. Turn out every idol. His place is on the heart's throne. Room to-day for Jesus! At the heart's door he knocks for admission. Rise! Draw back the bolt. Give Jesus welcome. He will be thy guest, and then he will graciously become thy royal host. All fulness dwells in Christ. To the sick he is a physician; to the hungry, bread; to the thirsty, water. In darkness he is a sun; in heat he is a shade. Stars and pearls, rocks and hills are drawn upon to describe his glory. Earth and air, sea and sky bring their noblest treasures and lay them at his feet. O Matchless Lily, O Fragrant Rose, O Clustering Vine, O Ineffable Christ, come and claim us to-day as thine own!

If Christ were the preacher to-day, this platform the mount, and you his audience, out of the fulness of his divine mind and the tenderness of his loving heart, he would say: "But seek ye first the kingdom of God and his righteousness, and all these things shall be added unto you." God help us all to do so here and now for his name's sake. Amen.

XV.

Anticipatory Blessings.

"*For thou preventest him with the blessings of goodness: thou settest a crown of pure gold on his head.*"—PSALM xxi. 3.

IN the preceding Psalm we have a prayer that David, who is going forth to war, may be victorious. In this Psalm we have a song of thanksgiving for the victory which has been won. Perowne describes the last Psalm as a litany before the king went forth to battle, and this one as the Te Deum on his return. The occasion which gave rise to the Psalm is variously understood. Some say that it celebrated the victory over Sennacherib; others that it is a song of thanksgiving for the recovery of Hezekiah. Still others consider it to be a song of rejoicing because of David's victory over the Ammonites, which 'ended in the capture of the royal city of Rabbah, the crown of whose king David put on his own brow. But without stopping to discuss this matter further in detail, these two Psalms are certainly complementary whatever the historical allusion.

A single remark on the word "prevent" will throw light upon its meaning in the text. Literally the word signifies to go before, to anticipate. This is the meaning alike of the Latin word from which it comes, and of the Hebrew word of which it is the translation. This also was the original meaning of the word prevent when our common translation of the Scriptures was made. We find this prayer in one of the old liturgies: "Prevent us, O Lord, in all our doings with thy most precious favor." The meaning of this petition is, that God would go before us or anticipate us in his mercy. Now, as we all know, the word prevent is used as meaning to stop, to hinder, to intercept. It is a sad commentary on our fallen human nature that the word should have so changed its meaning; for the changed meaning clearly shows that men usually go before one another not to help but to hinder and to hurt. "Words are things," as the fiery Mirabeau said in the French Assembly. There is a vast amount of history wrapped up in their changed meanings. Like Adam they have their fall. Moral qualities inhere in daily speech. The idea in this text is that God had gone before David, had anticipated him, had prepared blessings before they were asked or needed. This truth is taught whether we limit the application of the Psalm to some signal victory, or refer it to the whole sweep of God's providential dealings with David. God's providences as related to us emphasize the same truth. This fact suggests a general law in God's relations to man; it gives us this topic: The Anticipatory Blessings of God. .

1. These blessings are seen in creation—in creation generally, and in our own creation especially. The young of no creature come into the world so helpless as the young of the human species; but God so anticipates this fact that gentle hands and loving hearts make provision for this helplessness. Their manifest weakness appeals to our conscious strength. It has been said that "the undevout astronomer is mad." It may with equal truth be said that the undevout anatomist is mad. It is said that Galen, the celebrated physician, was at one time atheistically inclined, but that the careful study of the human frame, the usefulness of every part, the fitness of part to part, and the wonderful beauty of the whole, led him to question the truth of atheism, and finally to believe fully in God as Creator and Lord. He was a man of vast and varied attainments. Doubtless he was justified in speaking slightingly of the medical men of his time, and particularly of those in Rome, where during four years he won great applause for his skill as a practitioner and his success as an instructor. Eighty-three genuine

medical works by his hand are extant, and many
are supposed to have been lost. Tried by the
standards of our time his theories no doubt would
excite merriment, but for one thousand three hundred years his authority was law in the medical
profession. It is said that he wrote a hymn
in praise of the divine Creator. If we go for a
little way into particulars in the study of the human body we shall have many illustrations of God's
anticipated beneficence. Think for a moment of
the eye! At first it is needless, but all its parts are
even then perfect. God anticipates its subsequent
uses. A distinguished scholar has affirmed that an
examination of the eye is a cure for atheism. Dr.
Paley, whom some of us carefully studied in
academic days, reminds us that the eye is lodged in
a strong, deep, and bony socket composed of seven
different bones hollowed at their edges. It is shel-
tered by eyebrows, which are ingenious and beautiful arches of hair which render valuable service in
protecting the eyes from the moisture of the face.
The lid defends the eye in many ways, gently protecting it when open and then sweetly closing it in
sleep. To keep it clean a liquid is especially provided, and to carry off the superfluous brine a per-
foration is ingeniously prepared. The ear no less
than the eye is mechanically and scientifically
adapted to its office. Many writers call attention to

the fac; that we can find no machine in which such complicated and flexible contrivances are found as in the human neck. Think also of the contrivances in the fore-arm, and of the complicated arrangements to permit of the enlargement and contraction of the chest in breathing! Indeed, every joint and every part of the human system is a marvel of delicacy, power, and wisdom. We are wonderfully made. But of course I am not giving a lecture on anatomy, and so cannot go into these matters at length. The simple point here emphasized is that at the outset all these prospective contrivances were provided, God anticipating their subsequent use. Their relations as well as their adaptations are also anticipated. The eye is adapted to light, and the ear to sound; the wings of the bird to the air, and the fin of the fish to the water. These contrivances and designs prove the existence of the Contriver and Designer. They also illustrate the anticipatory goodness of the Designer; in a thousand ways they manifest his beneficence. He has added pleasure to the exercise of our faculties above what was necessary to their continued existence and intended function. Youth has pleasures of its own in its frolics and gambols; age, pleasures of its own, dozing in its arm-chair, or quietly engaged in its appropriate activities. God soothes the mind and comforts the eye by robing the earth in its green mantle, while he expresses his beautiful thoughts in flowers of many colors. However widely we traverse the realm of nature we shall find that God in creation has gone before us with the blessings of his goodness.

2. The same law is illustrated in Revelation. Men needed a revelation from God. Nature answered many of the deep questions of the human soul; but, when confronted by some of the profoundest problems of life, Nature is silent. The dying words of Goethe, "More light," express our need even when standing in the brightest light which Nature can give. God is a wise teacher; the impartation of his knowledge always bears a relation to our ability to receive. Christ had many things to tell the disciples which they were unable to bear. There is always a fulness of time in God's revelations and providences. It comes to pass, therefore, that it was always at "sundry times and in divers manners" that the knowledge of God came to men. Robertson reminds us that the sundry times "is literally sundry parts— sections, not of time, but of the manner of the revelation. God gave his revelation in parts, piecemeal, as you teach children to spell a word, letter by letter, syllable by syllable, adding all at last together. God had a word to spell—his own name. By degrees he did it." The Bible is like some ancient castle. Dr. Stowe reminds us that Warwick Castle viewed from the outside is an immense pile of disjointed work of

four or five centuries, and with many varieties of architecture, but within the apartments, although each is finished in the style of its own period, form a perfect and harmonious whole, making a desirable and convenient home. Cologne Cathedral on the banks of the "wide and winding Rhine," although founded in 1248, has just been completed. Its history is long and fascinating. The architect is unknown; probably he will never be known, but his design after hundreds of years is carried out in every particular. One thought dominates the structure in every part and harmonizes the entire conception. Such a majestic cathedral and historic castle is the Bible. It took sixteen centuries to make it; but its earlier portions anticipate and prepare for its later revelations. In the Old Testament we find the germ of those facts which blossom and bloom into precious truths, whose flower and fruitage we enjoy in the New Testament. Every portion of revelation was perfect for its place and time. Freeman has shown us, in his "Growth of the English Constitution," how the constitution of Britain up to to-day is the outgrowth of the earliest Saxon institutions of that land. So the full-blown flower of revelation is the development of the bud of divine teaching in the earliest history of the race. The doctrine of the Trinity, the hope of salvation, and the glory of the Messiah are all promised or implied in the teaching

14

of patriarchs and prophets at the very dawn of human history. Many men of many climes, and of varied degrees of intellect and spiritual culture, were employed in the preparation of the unique book which we call the Bible. Some of these men were prophets and poets; some were kings and some peasants; and some were shepherds and some were soldiers. They thus represented various grades of social life and of national growth, but all had their place and purpose in giving to the world God's full and glorious revelation of himself. Through the lofty arches of this great cathedral the idyllic song of the shepherd floats, and the imperial voice of the king thunders; here also the blended voices of evangelists and apostles echo, and all finally unite in ascriptions of praise to him who is the Child of the Manger and the Ancient of Days. The devout student discovers at every stage in this progressive revelation that God was going before men with the blessings of his goodness. There are questions which, without this revelation, we could never answer. What shall we think of God? Is there a life to come? How shall man be just with God? These questions uninspired wisdom could never answer. God implanted within us the longing to know something of himself, and the means by which that longing can be satisfied he also furnishes. He is ever going before us along the track of history and revelation. Traversing these highways of providence and redemption, we discover the footprints of the Son of God. As the loving John said to the impulsive Peter, in the gray dawn of the morning, near the shore of the Galilean Sea on which the Master was standing, "It is the Lord;" so the Christian student can say of every divine appointment in every dispensation. Echoing through the corridors of all the centuries the devout student hears the foot-beats of Jesus Christ. Revelation joins with creation in saying, "Thou preventest us with the blessings of thy goodness."

3. This beneficent law is illustrated especially in redemption. God is never taken by surprise; "Known unto God are all his works, from the beginning of the world." The first promise, given at the gate of Eden to our fallen parents, contains the Gospel as the seed contains the tree. In the garments given to cover the sinning pair was a hint at least of the spotless robe which is the righteousness of Christ. A ray of light from the distant cross of Calvary fell on their dark pathway as they walked from Eden's brightness. The cross was not an unexpected remedy for an unseen calamity. We are in danger of getting into deep water at this point, and of becoming entangled in the meshes of sublapsarianism and of supralapsarianism; but of this we may be sure: we ought always to have the

idea of the divine remedy in mind when we judge of the disaster which befell our race. It is certain that God anticipated the fall in the provisions of his mercy; certain that Christ was the Lamb slain before the foundation of the world; certain that God's knowledge anticipated the disaster as his loving power prepared the remedy. When there was no eye to pity, his eye pitied; when there was no hand outstretched to help, his was outstretched to save; before our sense of need came his provision of help.

And what is true of the provisions for the race as a whole is true in the conversion of each individual sinner. We should never have sought Christ if he had not first sought us. Christ sought Nathaniel under the fig tree, before Nathaniel sought him as his Saviour. Christ sought Matthew at the receipt of custom, while Matthew was intent only on the faithful performance of daily duty. Christ sought Zacchæus in the sycamore tree while he would have hid himself from the Lord behind its leafy branches. Christ sought the woman of Samaria at the well before she sought him as the Messiah. In the woman who was a sinner Christ sought and found the woman, although the Pharisees only sought and found the sinner. Christ was the Good Shepherd ever seeking the straying sheep. He is going before you to-day with the blessings of salvation. He came to you in the cradle. In the song prompted by a mother's heart and sung by her loving lips he was striving to win you to himself. He came to you in your school-days, saying to each boy and to each girl, "My son, my daughter, give me thine heart." He has come to you all in a thousand ways since with the same sweet message. In the blessings of health, of home, of a father's smile, of a mother's love, and of a child's trustful greeting, Jesus Christ has been coming with the blessings of his goodness. His warm love he offers you to-day. Oh, spurn not his mercy! Refuse not his anticipatory grace; but submit heart and life for time and for eternity into the hands of him who has loved you with an eternal love, and who waits to crown you with the blessings of his goodness.

4. The law of anticipatory blessings finds its illustration in Providence. All God's providential dealings are the blessings of his goodness. He waits to set a pure crown of gold on the head of every son and daughter of Adam. Our birth in this land is one of the blessings of his anticipating love; our birth in this particular age is an indisputable proof of that goodness; indeed, all his providences are such anticipations. It is true that "like as a father pitieth his children, so the Lord pitieth them that fear him;" it is true that "as one whom his mother comforteth, so will I comfort you;" it is true that, "all things work together for good to them that love

God." Our blessed Lord is preparing us for what
he has prepared for us. We are a prepared people
for a prepared mansion and crown. Look over your
past life, and you will see how this law has been illustrated. Observe to-day your present experiences,
and you will know some day just why you have had
them as they are. To-day we are to sit at the table
of the Lord. The ordinance of the Lord's Supper is
an illustration of the Lord's considerate goodness.
He knew that we would need such a help in our
spiritual lives; this ordinance he gave us to be
observed in remembrance of him. The Lord's Baptism sets forth the beginning of the new life in
Christ; the Lord's Supper the continuance of that
life by his grace and power. The Lord's Baptism
is to be observed but once, as it is the symbol of the
new birth; the Lords' Supper is to be observed often,
as it is the symbol of our daily dependence upon God
for strength and growth. The Good Shepherd ever
goeth before his sheep and leadeth them. He leads,
he never drives. There is no pathway, however
thorny, which we must tread which he has not
trodden; there is no cross, however heavy, which we
must bear that he has not borne. Is death before
us? He has gone through the valley and made it
luminous by his presence. Must we enter the tomb?
There he once lay, and therefrom he came forth in
triumph. Do we need a mansion in glory? He

anticipates the need, saying: "I go to prepare a place for you." Do we need a friend at the right hand of God? "He ever liveth to make intercession for them." The Psalm from which the text is taken is, as we have seen, a triumphal ode. It speaks of a crown of pure gold. But a loftier song than this psalm shall be sung when we chant, "Thanks be to God, which giveth us the victory through our Lord Jesus Christ." A nobler crown shall be worn, if we be faithful unto death and let no man take our crown, for there is laid up for us a triple crown, the crown of righteousness, the crown of life, and the crown of glory.

XVI.

Watching Ibim There.

"*And sitting down, they watched him there.*"—MATT. xxvii. 36.

THE "sitting down" spoken of in the text seems to indicate a temporary change in the feeling and conduct of the crucifiers of our Lord. The attitude here described is the first breathing-place which they had in their work of death; it marks the first moment of serious reflection in the dizzy whirl of their rage. Alike before and after this time all was fierce passion and bitter railing; now there is a lull in the storm which had swept on so wildly. As the commanding voice of Christ once sounded over the Sea of Galilee, hushing its wild waves into stillness, so now the eloquent silence of the patient Sufferer hushes the turbulent sea of human passions; and, of this occasion, as of that, it might be said, "there was a great calm."

"Silence is vocal, if we listen well," says an American poet; and truly this awe-inspiring silence, together with the fear-inducing darkness which soon followed, overshadowing the land from the sixth hour to the ninth hour, speak volumes to every listening heart of the greatness of him who dies. It is said that murderers are drawn by a strange fascination to the spot where they have committed the foul deed, even though their coming may expose them to detection and death; and perhaps something like this feeling may have prompted some to the watching spoken of in the text.

1. Let us, in the first place, study the watchers of that strange sight—"*they* watched him there." Who are the persons meant by the pronoun "they" in the text? There were large numbers of persons at or near the cross. From all parts of the land they were accustomed to go to Jerusalem to be present at the Passover. Josephus has, perhaps with some exaggeration, said that often not fewer than two and a half to three millions were present on Passover occasions. The increased excitement attending the death of One who had awakened loving gratitude in the hearts of many, and hatred in the hearts of many others, could not fail to attract an unusually large number about the cross of Christ. Many gazed with comparative indifference that day on the dying Sufferer, who afterward learned to regard his name as the most blessed name on earth or in heaven. In that crowd are persons of many classes and conditions; they are there with various motives and

with contradictory emotions. But the tumultuous crowd can be arranged practically under a few classes. Prominent among those about the cross and gazing on that dreadful scene are the Roman soldiers. They were not much more than mere machines; they had to obey orders—"theirs not to reason why." They were there for a practical object; there was danger lest the friends of Jesus should come and take him down from the cross, and thus preserve his life. We are told that Josephus had a friend who was thus taken down and who lived; and many similar cases have occurred even after three hours had been spent upon the cross. The wounds in crucifixion were not necessarily mortal, hence the necessity of watching the crucified. There were four soldiers, a centurion, and three others as an official guard. They watched with little concern, certainly with little sympathy. But they were free from all the prejudices of the Jew, and they were more open to the influences of the truth. Throughout the whole trial and crucifixion they manifest a candor and manliness as gratifying as unexpected. Were it not for their base and unaccountable part in endeavoring to conceal the resurrection, their record in connection with the crucifixion would be comparatively noble. Because the Jews had not the power of life and death, the Romans conducted the crucifixion according to the forms of their law. It must, therefore, be attended to with the precision peculiar to these law-observing Romans. As parts of the chain of Roman order which girded the world, these Roman soldiers sat watching the expiring Saviour. They could not remain entirely unmoved; for this was no ordinary execution. They had seen many criminals put to death; but they had never witnessed so wonderful a "malefactor" as was Jesus. Familiar with bloodshed, they never before were moved as now. A thoughtful Roman must have wondered at the opposition manifested toward Jesus. Why should the Jews insist upon the death of Jesus? What evil had he done? The thought of that harmless Nazarene rising against Cæsar was sheer folly. Every intelligent Roman knew that such an assertion was utterly unfounded. Even an ordinary soldier must have had thoughts like these. Why this lying testimony and fierce rage against the meek and lowly One? Why this unappeasable clamor for his death? Questions like these must have suggested themselves to these Roman watchers.

Not in vain did these soldiers watch him there. Although darkness was gathering about the cross, light was dawning upon some of these Roman hearts. Not in vain were the dying words of Christ spoken. Even at the moment of their utterance they were awakening a response in the heart of the centurion;

even then was the promise fulfilled, "I shall give thee the heathen for thine inheritance, and the uttermost parts of the earth for thy possession." Before entering the portal of death, Christ opened the door of life to the guilty robber; and, dying in shame, he gave the hope of life and glory to the Roman centurion. Gaze on, ye Roman soldiers! for you also is this Jesus dying: no Pharisee shall shut you out from the kingdom of God! Soldiers, victorious under the eagles of Rome, you may come off more than conquerors through the blood and under the banner of Immanuel!

Another class conspicuously present is made up of chief priests and Pharisees. So frequent and so violent has been the denunciation of these that one feels it to be almost a virtue not to denounce them. The sermons of John the Baptist were filled with solemn warnings against this "generation of vipers;" and no discourses were ever spoken in any age or language so terrible with "woes" as the last public addresses of Christ against the Scribes and Pharisees. One is almost appalled as he hears the scathing rebukes which came from the lips of the loving Saviour. These priests and Pharisees were very religious in connection with the crucifixion. All men must have observed the sanctity of their faces and the punctilious propriety of their manners. All impiety must have been rebuked in their presence, and all evil-doers must have hung their heads in very shame. But, however these outwardly religious Pharisees might impose on man, they could not deceive Christ. He laid bare their inmost souls, revealing their hypocrisy and exposing their inordinate self-righteousness. So religious were they that they would not enter the judgment-hall of Pilate lest they might be defiled. But they presumed to enter into the presence of God with their lying words and blasphemous prayers. They could suborn witnesses; they could falsely testify, using the selfish Pilate as their tool, and making the sinless Christ their victim. No wonder these Pharisees hated Jesus; no wonder they plotted against him; no wonder they crucified him; and no wonder they now sit down and watch him there. Until darkness loves light, until sin loves holiness, and Satan God, Pharisees must hate Christ. Gaze on, ye murderous Scribes and Pharisees! Ye will crucify your own Messiah—him of whom your prophets wrote; him whom it has been your greatest joy and your highest hope to expect.

There, too, in silence and horror sit the rank and file of the people who made themselves hoarse in shouting, "Away with him, crucify him!" We pity them more for their folly than we blame them for their crime. They were the dupes of designing rulers; they were ready a little before to shout "Ho-

sanna," and now just as ready to cry, " Crucify him !"
Here are those who spat upon him and smote him
with the palms of their hands. Surely their hearts
now relent. See that bowed head, that lacerated
back, and those bleeding hands and feet! At that
sight the sun hid his face. When Christ was born
the glory of noonday illumined the darkness of
midnight; when Christ dies the darkness of midnight takes the place of the brightness of noonday.
When Christ dies the very earth shudders and
quakes—the rocks rend and the graves open. Amid
this crowd of " common people," who once heard
Christ gladly, God had many precious jewels—
jewels which are soon to take the place of that
crown of thorns on the brow of Christ. But we
may believe that still the chief priests and the Pharisees looked on the dying Lord with only thoughts of
hate in their hearts. There was murder in their
hearts; there was murder in their faces. There was
triumph, too, in heart and face; their plans were successful; and that haughty young Jew who would not
bow to their mandates is brought low.' He is in the
agonies of death; they are in ecstasies of joy. He
is under the frown of God's wrath; they, in their
own estimation, are in the enjoyment of his approv-
ing smile. But it is almost certain that their joy
is strangely intermingled with fear; an indefinable
terror chills their hearts. What if he be the Son of

God? What if his blood should come upon us and our children? This thought is the handwriting on the wall of their souls which suggests a fearful looking-for of judgment and fiery indignation. The painter who could catch and portray all these varying and conflicting emotions now upon their faces would immortalize himself and his art. It is almost impossible for us to look upon the Pharisees gloating in hellish glee over the dying Jesus and speak of them in terms of moderation.

Others also are watching that strange sight who may not be omitted in this enumeration: "And many women were there, beholding afar off, which followed Jesus from Galilee, ministering unto him."

Last at the cross and first at the tomb, these faithful women stand before the world as true heroines, whose devotion nothing could lessen, whose faithfulness was as loyal as it was unselfish, and whose love many waters could not drown. Farther off in position, they were nearer in heart; undemonstrative in action, they were unchanging in affection. Among them was Mary Magdalene. Once she had bowed under the sevenfold power of Satan, now she is restored to her right mind. Still may she gaze with tearful sympathy and saddened joy; she had received much, she loves much. There, too, was the mother Mary, through whose soul the sword had gone. There were many others like Martha and Mary, whose hospitality he had shared, and who gave him their personal affection. There were many in this group of disciples who silently and with breaking hearts watched his agony. They are scattered sheep; their shepherd is smitten. Some stand near the cross; some are mingling with Pharisees and soldiers; more look on from a distance. One almost rebukes them for their cowardly desertion of their Master in his hour of sorrow; one almost wishes that they had rushed into danger, even into death, to fulfil their boastful declarations of love. In that company are those who have received his manifold benefactions. Their eyes are now blinded with tears and their hearts are breaking with grief. So strangely mysterious are all these events, so sudden are the surprises of the times, and so baffled and conflicting are their hopes, that they know not what opinions to cherish nor what courses to pursue. It was theirs in after-times to show the world how brave, how noble, how divine frail human nature could become when constrained by the love and inspired by the power of Jesus Christ. Theirs it was afterward to gaze on the cross with transports of joy and to catch the inspiration of him who hung thereon, and then to go to the ends of the earth, telling the story of his love, enduring the shame of his cross, and rejoicing to suffer and to die with him.

2. Let us observe, in the second place, the august Person whom they watched there—"they watched *him* there." There were three crosses on Calvary, and on each cross hung a sufferer. But one only was the subject of thought and the special object of sight. The Galilean challenged the attention of all, whether in love or hate, in sorrow or in joy. "Never man spake like this man," was the testimony of the messengers of the Pharisees who were seeking to arrest Jesus. We may also add, never did man love like this man, and never did man evoke love as did this man. Jesus himself said, shortly before his crucifixion: "And I, if I be lifted up from the earth, will draw all men unto me;" and even while he is suspended on the cross his prophecy is fulfilled. What means that strange fascination which rivets all eyes on the dying Jesus? What strange power is it that invests the humiliated Christ with this kingly attraction? What mysterious influence was it that compelled the centurion to exclaim, "Truly this was the Son of God!" To him long before prophets directed their gaze; his day Abraham saw afar off, and the sight rejoiced his heart. To serve him a star marks a new path in the heavens; to him the wise men came from the East bringing their gifts of wealth, of learning, and of love, and laid them at his feet. To him blindness rolled its sightless eyeballs when his approaching footsteps were

15

heard.   To him sorrow turned its weeping eyes and
lifted its broken heart; and to him winds and waves
rendered ready obedience.   To him angels came
from heaven ministering in his hour of agony; and
against him hell directed its deadliest shafts, and
from him Satan, baffled, turned away.   And now
in his deepest humiliation to him all eyes are turned
as never to men in highest greatness.   Is he only a
man who thus challenges and receives the wonder-
ing gaze, the loving admiration, and the profound
adoration or the rancorous hatred of all those who
watched him in life and who gazed upon him in
death?   The very stones cry out a thousand times
no—he is man; he is God; he is the eternal Word
made flesh, and through that veil of flesh the pre-
existing glory shines.   He is the Child of the Manger; he is the Ancient of Days; he is the Son of
man; he is the Son of God.   Seeming defeat, real
humiliation, and an ignominious death cannot conceal his awful majesty, his sublime personality, his
august deity.   The world has ever since been drawn
to him in tenderest love, or at least in admiring
wonder.   Men have attempted in vain with the
fullest scholarship and the greatest genius to write
his life.   Jews confess admiration for his character,
and Mohammedans place him above all the prophets.
Geikie in his introduction to his "Life of Christ"
reminds us that the myriad-minded Shakespeare paid

lowliest reverence in passage after passage to Jesus
Christ; that Galileo, Kepler, Bacon, Newton, and
Milton exalt the name of Jesus above every other
name; that Spinoza calls Christ the symbol of the
divine wisdom, and Kant the symbol of ideal perfection; that Goethe is amazed at the reflected splendor
of divinity which shines in the Gospels; that Rous-
seau calls the books of the philosophers petty compared with the gospels, and adds, "If the death of
Socrates be that of a sage, the life and death of Jesus
are those of a God;" that Thomas Carlyle calls Jesus
of Nazareth "our divinest symbol;" that the exqui-
site genius of Herder says that "Jesus Christ is, in
the noblest and in the most perfect sense, the realized
ideal of humanity;" that Napoleon, who strode the
world like a Colossus, says among other striking
things of Jesus, "I think I understand somewhat
of human nature, and I tell you . . . that Jesus
Christ was more than man. Alexander, Cæsar,
Charlemagne, and myself founded great empires;
but upon what did the creations of our genius
depend? Upon force. Jesus alone founded his
empire upon love, and to this very day millions
would die for him." And to illustrate this great
thought further Geikie quotes this magnificent sentence from Jean Paul Richter: "The life of Christ
concerns him who, being the holiest among the
mighty, the mightiest among the holy, lifted with

his pierced hand empires off their hinges, and turned
the stream of centuries out of its channel, and still
governs the ages." O mystery of mysteries, Christ
manifest in the flesh! O abounding grace and
matchless love! The eternal God in the garb of
man, the sinless Christ dying for a sinful race! O
my soul! in wonder, adoration, and love, gaze on
him and him alone; gaze on him until thou shalt
exalt him as thy prophet, king, and priest on earth,
and until he shall become the theme of thy song in
heaven!

3. We notice also the place where they saw him—
" They watched him *there*." There on the cross they
watched him; there in his weakness and humiliation. Not on a cross do men love to see their heroes.
Rather in the strife of conflict and in the flush of
victory do they love to gaze on heroes, but not so
with Christ. Not to him driving out from the temple those who made it a place of merchandise does
the world turn its eye; not to him stilling the sea
and raising the dead. Glorious as he is always and
everywhere, when we see him on the cross we forget
all else and adore him most as the Lamb that was
slain. Many paintings and descriptions there are
of the cross, but there never was a true one. There
was a glory and there was a shame attaching to the
cross which no painter can reproduce. There are
always given him a halo of heavenly glory and a

calmness of features which are strangely unlike the
awful reality. We can never understand the awful
weight of woe which he bore as the sinner's substitute on the cross of Calvary. We do not know fully
what is meant by the words, " He bore our sins in his
own body on the tree." But though we cannot understand all, and would not minutely describe all that
we can understand, we can still know that it is in
his character as sufferer, as vicarious sacrifice, that
we most adore him. Hating the sin which made
him die, we can magnify the love which made the
sacrifice. We are lost in the mystery of godliness
as we strive to fathom the awful depths and to scale
the lofty heights of wisdom and love which the cross
suggests; but we can still rejoice in the assurance
of the heavenly blessings which the cross imparts.·
Watching him there light is thrown upon all the
past appointments of God; the Old Testament thus
becomes radiant with meaning and resplendent with
light. Secular history becomes intelligible. The
deepest questions of the human heart are answered,
and God is seen to be just and yet the justifier of
him who believes in Jesus. Building our studio on
Calvary the events of Providence and history become
a divine harmony, although standing anywhere else
they would be confusion and chaos. The cross is.the
pivot around which all the events of history revolve;
it is the centre of the universe; it is the key which

unlocks the mystery of human history and destiny.
At the cross the beautiful language of the Psalmist
is illustrated:

> "Mercy and truth are met together,
> Righteousness and peace have kissed each other."

The original beholders of this sad sight are gone.
Brave soldiers, haughty Pharisees, and gentle
women have blended in common dust; but they
were types of all subsequent beholders, and as such
they still live. The world ever since has sat
watching him there. A mysterious spell has bound
men, whether in love or hate, to the cross of Christ.
The soldiers still live. They, in their cold and
mechanical performance of duty, are reproduced in
the historian who writes of Christ and his work with
the coolness or even hatred of Gibbon and others; in
the philosopher who discusses him with the assumed
indifference or sentimental interest of Renan. But
their indifference is seldom real. Their effort to
appear unconcerned shows their deep anxiety. They
cannot leave Christ alone. They keep writing about
him. Why are they anxious to overthrow his work?
Oh, what a power there is in watching Christ there!
Well might Paul glory in Christ crucified—as the
power of God, power to awaken the tenderest love,
power to evoke the direst hate. A touch-stone is
this view of Christ drawing and repelling men and

always revealing what is in their heart. From Celsus and Porphyry to infidels of to-day men have gazed there. They could not help it; they must look, and like the Roman centurion some commencing in cold indifference have ended by exclaiming, "Truly this was the Son of God." Others, like Julian the Apostate, may say in their pride: "Wretch, I will crush thee;" but like him they will have to say in their weakness, "O Galilean, thou hast conquered!" Christ is set for the rising and falling of many, and if men do not rise higher by the sight they must fall lower. Who to-day is sitting down and watching him there with cold indifference? It cannot be with indifference. If the sight does not melt, it will freeze; if it does not soften, it will harden. The sight of the crucified One rent flinty rocks and broke proud Roman hearts, and shall one this morning view that sight and remain unsubdued? Oh, " behold the man" until your souls bow before him with the prayer, "Lord, save me or I perish."

Pharisees, sometimes within the Church, and oftener without the Church, have in every age sat gazing on Christ. Sometimes they are in the Church great sticklers for words and forms—the anise, mint, and cumin, ardent champions of the letter—while they entirely forget in their conduct toward their brethren the spirit of the Gospel and the weightier matters of the law. Sometimes out of the Church they stand aloof from Christian duty and can only criticise those whose shoe-latchets they are not worthy to unloose. They will not go in themselves and they would prevent all others from going in. Are there any such sitting down and watching Christ this morning? Is that the spirit which his holy life and painful death teach? Fling from you the tattered garb of your own righteousness and come in your poverty to Christ; he will make you rich, clothing you, humbling you, and sending you away in your right mind.

The loving disciples and the gentle women who stood beholding him there have never ceased to watch him. Now in caves and rocks, now in Alpine valleys and on many hill-tops faithful men and women have in all ages stood up for Jesus. The bravest and truest the world has ever seen were those who knew Christ and his self-sacrificing love, who feared him and knew no other fear. We have read of the brave three hundred who devoted themselves to death at Thermopylæ for the salvation of their country; we have read of the Locrian king who, when his son had broken the laws, the punishment of which was that both eyes should be put out, gave one of his own, thus enduring a part of his child's suffering; we all know of the lovely English queen who sucked the poison from her husband's wound, though she knew death was her reward. But never were sacrifices like Christ's; never was devotion like that of his followers. God bless those humble disciples of Christ who, unknowing and unknown, are living and laboring for Christ. God bless those faithful and gentle women who, in whatever circle they move, from the highest to the lowest, know how to serve their Master, beholding him until they are transformed into his image.

And sitting down in this house you have been watching him there for this hour. Some Pharisee has been rebuked. Some disciple has been encouraged, and some careless ones have been awakened. I now ask, "What will you do with Jesus who is called Christ?" He who was sent to prepare the way of the Lord and make his paths straight, gives the right reply: "Behold the Lamb of God, which taketh away the sin of the world."

XVII

Ⴀhe Dead and the Living Christ.

"I am he that liveth, and was dead: and, behold, I am alive for evermore, amen; and have the keys of hell and of death."—
REVELATION i. 18.

THESE are the words of the glorified Jesus to the exiled John. We have in this connection a magnificent description of Christ as he appeared in glory, standing in the midst of the seven candles, clothed with a long garment, and girt with a golden girdle. His hair was white as snow, his eyes were as a flame of fire, his feet like unto fine brass, and his voice like the sound of many waters. In his right hand he had seven stars, and from his mouth went a sharp two-edged sword, and his countenance was like the sun in its dazzling splendor. John, overawed by the sight, fell at his feet as if he were dead; but the glorified one lays his hand tenderly upon the apostle, exhorting him not to fear, and assuring him that though he, the triumphant Saviour, was dead, he is now alive for evermore, and has the

keys of hell and death. We are not surprised that
the apostle, recognizing the presence of a divine
being, is greatly alarmed; neither are we surprised
that when he recognizes in this glorious personage
the Lord Jesus, whom years before he had known
so well and loved so tenderly, his fears are allayed,
and his soul is filled with peace and joy.

1. The text teaches us that Christ was tempora-
rily dead. This description at once identifies the
glorious Personage who thus appeared to the astonished apostle. To none other would this remarkable
description apply. Jesus Christ had been truly put to
death; he was certainly dead. On this point there can
be no doubt. This account carries us back at once
to the history of Christ in the gospels. After he had
uttered his seventh saying upon the cross his head
sank upon his breast, and the Lord of life and glory
was dead. The marvel to all who were familiar
with his crucifixion was that he should die so
speedily. He had been on the cross but about six
hours; and we know that often the crucified lingered
two or three days before death came to relieve their
sufferings. How shall we account for our Lord's
speedy death? Several considerations enter into this
answer. The exhaustion incident to that long and
checkered "night in which he was betrayed," has its
part in this answer. We have only to think of the
sorrowful passover, of the bloody sweat, of the cruel

arrest, of the illegal trials before Annas and Caia-
phas, of the arraignment before Pilate and Herod, of
the brutal scourging, of the taunting mockeries, and
of the physical pain on the cross, to discover reasons
for his death so unexpectedly soon. There was also
a deeper reason, which mere natural causes will not
explain. Our Lord was bearing our sins in his own
body on the tree; in the hiding of his Father's face,
as evidenced by his own agonizing cry, there was a
sorrow which no human tongue can explain. Mere
physical causes will not account for the early death
of one whose proper life gave sound health and a
vigorous body. It may be true, as Dr. William
Stroud and others have argued, that he died of literal
rupture of the heart. This supposition will explain
solemn prophecies in the 22d Psalm, as well as some
of his own exclamations while upon the cross. This
idea has received the indorsement of some critics
who are among the ablest physicians, as well as the
most reverent believers of our time.

We know that the Romans were accustomed to
allow the bodies of the crucified to remain on the
cross until they were devoured by birds of prey, or
wasted away by decomposition. This fact was one
of the elements of the fearful degradation of this
form of death. But by a special law the Jews took
down the bodies of the crucified before sunset; it is
certain that this course would be pursued in this case,

as the next day was not only the Sabbath, but the Sabbath of the great Passover Feast. The next day was " an high day," and no time is to be lost, as but a few hours at most remain before the sun shall set, as it is now fast westering. We are told that the authorities besought Pilate that the death of the victims might be hastened, so that there might be no desecration of the sanctity of the Sabbath by permitting the dead to remain upon their crosses upon that day. Pilate yielded and gave the necessary orders, and soldiers were sent at once to give them effect. The action of these soldiers in hastening the death of those upon the cross was called a *coup de grace;* as the blow of the heavy mallet which the soldiers used in breaking the legs of those upon the cross resulted in immediate death. The soldiers break the legs of the robbers, but we are told that when they came to Jesus " they brake not his legs," and the reason assigned is that they " saw that he was dead already." This is one proof of the actual death of Jesus. These soldiers little knew that they were fulfilling a prophecy which was uttered fifteen hundred years before—a prophecy which the evangelist John records, " a bone of him shall not be broken." But there was a bare possibility that Jesus might have swooned and that he was not really dead. To make assurance doubly sure, " one of the soldiers with a spear pierced his side, and forthwith came thereout blood and water." These soldiers must faithfully perform their duty. This scene produced a profound impression on the mind of the sensitive John. Years after, when he records the event in his gospel, the solemn occasion is reproduced in all its vivid details; and still later, when writing in his epistle, he says: "This is he that came by water and blood, even Jesus Christ; not by water only, but by water and blood."

We shall not stop here to discuss the physiological details which this solemn fact suggests, nor to dwell upon the arguments which have arisen in connection with it, but we cannot help noticing that this incident fulfilled another prophecy, of which the same evangelist speaks: "They shall look on him whom they pierced." The flowing of the water and the blood is of great importance in establishing beyond a doubt the reality of Christ's death. The spear-thrust did not cause his death. He was already dead; but if he had not been dead that spear-thrust would certainly have produced death. By anticipation two heresies which afterward sprang up were refuted by these solemn occurrences: one heresy was that he only swooned; the other, that of the Docetæ, that his body was not real, but only apparent. It would seem as if there was a divine design in the anticipation and refutation of these two heresies. He could appeal to his own consciousness for the truth of the solemn statements which he makes. His positive and repeated statements of the facts connected with the spear-thrusts and the flowing stream of blood and water leave no doubt as to the fact that our Lord had a veritable body and that that body was truly dead. Yes, the Son of God, the Lord of Life and Glory, is dead. Shall he be buried in a malefactor's grave? Again remarkable providences prevent this humiliation. God proposes to give honor to his Son, who has now completed the work of atonement. A Jewish senator and a Jewish rabbi appear upon the scene. The disciples timidly and surprisedly watch their approach. The wealthy Joseph of Arimathea goes to Pilate to secure the body. His request is granted, and Nicodemus and he assist in taking it tenderly from the cross and preparing it for burial. Wealth will furnish appropriate spicery and love will give becoming gentleness. Lovingly, even if hastily, the body is wrapped in the sheet thus secured. Joseph will open his new and costly tomb for its reception. In that tomb it is laid, and thus another ancient prophecy is fulfilled. The sun goes down, the darkness deepens, and Mary of Magdala and the other Mary sit over against the sepulchre where the Lord is laid. In that rocky tomb, motionless, dead, the mighty Redeemer lies. No child of Adam was more truly dead than was the Lord of Life and Glory. Well may he

say to the apostle John, reminding him of the scenes
he had witnessed at the cross, "I am he . . . that
was dead."

2. But we observe, in the next place, that this same
Jesus is "alive for evermore." So he affirms in his
interview with the disciple whom he loved. Death
is no more to claim him as its victim. Evermore he
lives to bless his people and to comfort them with
this glorious assurance. In that wonderful chapter,
the 15th of I. Corinthians, the apostle Paul makes the
death and life of Christ the very substance of his
gospel. He affirms "that Christ died for our sins
according to the scriptures, and that he was buried,
and that he rose again the third day according to
the scriptures." The fact of the resurrection of
Christ is stated to the apostle John as a reason why
he should not fear. This apostle was the first person
in the world who ever believed that Christ had risen
from the dead. On that glorious morning when he
ran, together with Peter, to the tomb and beheld that
the tomb was empty, that the napkin was folded in
a place by itself, that every indication showed that the
tomb had not been rifled, and that the Lord had not
made a hasty exit, an incipient faith in the great
event dawned in his heart. That early faith,
strengthened by the subsequent appearances of Christ
during the forty days, is now emphasized as he be-
holds in his · matchless glory the same Jesus whom

once he had seen laid in the tomb. John is especially
the evangelist who spoke of Christ as "the Life."
Again and again he speaks of him as the Life and
the Light of men; he also presents him as the Resurrection and the Life. Fittingly, therefore, is he
now chosen to publish the fact that Christ is alive
for evermore. Our Lord affirms, with a solemn
amen, the fact of his possession of unending life.
This strong affirmation is also quite in harmony
with the records given by this same apostle. Again
and again he reports the solemn utterances of his
Lord, preceding them with his familiar truly, truly,
or his amen, amen.

This appearance of Christ carries us once more
back to the Gospel narrative. We remember the
new tomb with the great stone placed at its mouth.
We remember the placing of Cæsar's great seal and
the appointment of the night-watch. We see the
soldiers as they pace to and fro during the solemn
hours guarding the tomb of the mighty dead; but we
learn later that the grave is empty and that the Lord
of Life and Glory has burst the bands of death and
has overturned the throne of the grim despot who so
long had reigned without a rival in the regions of
despair and death. No human eye witnessed the
glorious resurrection; it has been well said that often
God's sublimest works are wrought in silence and
secrecy; but of the resurrection there can be no more

16

doubt than of the death. If the testimony of these witnesses cannot be taken as conclusive, then no testimony of any witnesses can ever make any historical event certain. The clumsy story of the soldiers and of the chief priests can impose upon no student of the narrative. Christ's resurrection is the great, majestic, and sublime fact of Christianity. The corner-stone of the Christian Church is laid in his grave. On this glad Easter morning we hail him as the Conqueror of sin, the Vanquisher of death, and the Ransomer from the grave. His resurrection is the keystone in the sublime arch of revelation and Christianity. The resurrection of Christ has exalted the poetry, the music, the sculpture, the painting, and the literature of the world. It is the proof of all Christ's assertions concerning himself. He staked all on that event. It is the conclusive evidence of all his prophecies concerning himself. It also emphasizes and glorifies the story of his incarnation, of his perfect life, and of his atoning death. The apostles were willing to set that fact forth as a sufficient evidence of the truth they preached. We follow their example. Dr. Boardman, in his volume on "The Epiphanies of the Risen Lord," has beautifully said: "The resurrection stands forth in the apostolic theology as the epitome and very label of Christianity itself. And well it may; for it involves the whole story of the Incarnation. He who has risen must have died, and he who has died must have lived, and he who has lived must have been born. Jerusalem's empty tomb proves Bethlehem's holy manger. And so it comes to pass that belief in the resurrection of Christ is the touch-stone of the Christian faith, the key to the kingdom of heaven." The apostle Paul has taught us that if Christ be not risen, our faith is vain. The resurrection of Christ gives us a living Saviour. Others before had been dead and were brought to life, but they now sleep in death. Lazarus is dead; the daughter of Jairus is dead; the son of the widow of Nain is dead, but Christ is alive for evermore. Other religions had their great leaders, but they died to live no more; but Christianity's Founder rises to live for evermore. We worship a living, and not a dead, Christ. The dead Christ is unwelcome in art and still more unwelcome in religion. We shall not make less of the cross on which the Lord of Glory dies, but we shall make more of the grave from which he rises in triumph. If we are reconciled to God by the death of his Son, we are still more fully saved by his life. From the living Lord we derive our divine life. With these precious memories and exalted hopes we welcome with garlands of flowers and songs of triumph the living and loving Lord on this Easter morning. We give him a carpet of flowers for his once pierced feet; we give him a crown of glory instead of the crown of thorns;

and because he lives, we know that we shall live also.

His resurrection accounts for the existence of the church. The Christian Church has been and is; that fact no amount of infidelity can deny. The Christian Church has transformed the world; that fact no amount of infidelity can deny. Canon Farrar has finely shown how the Church has regenerated literature, sanctified marriage, ennobled woman, conquered the world, and glorified God. But how can we account for the Christian Church, except as we admit the resurrection of the Lord? The first preachers went forth affirming their faith in the resurrection. Were they deceived? Who can so believe? Were they deceivers? Who dare so affirm? The resurrection of the Lord Jesus is a sufficient explanation of the existence of the Church. Deny the resurrection, and you cannot account for the Church. This fact any man may safely affirm in the presence of any student of history. You may challenge any man who denies the resurrection of Christ to account for the existence of the Church. No sensible man will accept the challenge. The resurrection is the crowning miracle of Christianity. If it be true, all other miracles are credible. To this miracle the apostles constantly appealed; to it we to-day appeal with the utmost confidence. The apostle Paul said, " If Christ be not risen your faith is vain," but he was able to add the glorious announcement, " Now is Christ risen." This truth has resounded throughout the world; it is really the creation of a new heaven and earth. Death is discrowned; the gates of life and glory are open. From the night of death the sun of a new life has arisen upon the world. The brightness of that triumphant morning now shines over the earth. The apostles attached the greatest importance to the preaching of the resurrection. To be a witness to this truth was one function of their calling. On the day of Pentecost the apostle Peter said: " This Jesus hath God raised up, whereof we all are witnesses." Later, when questioned regarding a miracle which had been performed, the same apostle said: " Be it known unto you all, and to all the people of Israel, that by the name of Jesus Christ of Nazareth, whom ye crucified, whom God raised from the dead, even by him doth this man stand here before you whole." It was said of the apostles a little later that with great power they gave witness of the resurrection. Than Paul's reasoning in I. Corinthians, 15th chapter, nothing can be more logical or sublime. Every reader of the Gospel has observed what a great proportion of space is given to the events of the three days preceding and following Christ's death—almost as much space as is given to the three preceding years of his life. These facts certainly are remarkably suggestive.

3. Christ is shown by this text to be Sovereign over death and Hades. He is here represented as having the key of death; he holds the key to the vast realms of darkness and death. The word here rendered "hell" refers to the under-world, the abode of spirits, the region of the dead. This imagery of a gate and keys was natural in a country with walled cities and gates. Death is represented as having reigned in that gloomy abode. He was the inexorable tyrant, the autocratic potentate. No tears could move him, no prayers could bribe him, as he marched forward to receive his victims. Only two in the whole history of our race passed into glory without going through the gates of death. But once, there entered a strange visitor into that dark realm: he seemed to yield to the power of the tyrant, but only to make that tyrant's overthrow more conspicuous. Death was astonished; Death was discrowned; Death was destroyed by the Lord of Life and Glory. We now have nothing to fear. We are Christ's and Christ is King. Death lies vanquished at his feet. That dark portal can open only by Christ's permission. We need not fear to enter a world which he entered, and from which he returned in triumph. Because he lives we shall live also. Standing by the empty grave of Christ we take up the triumphant words of the apostle: "O death, where is thy sting? O grave,

where is thy victory? But thanks be to God, which giveth us the victory through our Lord Jesus Christ."

This doctrine of the resurrection, then, is a striking proof of our Lord's divinity. If the resurrection be true, our Lord's divinity is assured. Disprove the resurrection, and you rob him of the crown of his divinity; accept the resurrection, and you must crown him Lord of all. The apostles Peter and Paul indorse these statements: Paul affirms that Christ was "declared to be the Son of God with power by the resurrection from the dead." And on Mars Hill he affirms that God will judge the world by Christ because "He hath given assurance unto all men in that he hath raised him from the dead." Christ's whole life was a testimony to his divine character and mission; but his resurrection is the crowning glory of that testimony. He foretold his resurrection; he affirmed that he had power to lay down his life and to take it again. The resurrection is the proof of his character as a true prophet and as a divine Being, for he claimed the power to raise himself from the dead, and if he did raise himself he was God. He rose from the dead; therefore, he is God. The atonement was finished, not upon the cross of Calvary, but in the tomb of Joseph. Finely has his resurrection been called "God's amen and the hallelujah of humanity." If his work had not been completed and his atonement accepted, he had never risen from the tomb.

The resurrection is also a prophecy of our resurrection. Christ won this victory not for himself alone. Through the open grave he has made a way along which all his redeemed may pass. The Good Shepherd goeth before his sheep. Our resurrection depends upon his. When men say that the scientific objections are such that they cannot believe in the doctrine of the resurrection, we have simply to ask them, Did Jesus rise? That is a question of fact. Is it true? There are, all admit, difficulties in the doctrine of our resurrection. They are inexplicable; but were there not also difficulties in the resurrection of Christ? The difficulties in the case of a general resurrection are not greater, from a strictly scientific point of view, than those in the case of the resurrection of Jesus. To believe that he died and rose again is scientifically as difficult as to believe that we die and may rise again. He who denies that the dead can rise must also deny that Christ did rise. "But now is Christ risen." Then we, too, may rise. Empty as was Joseph's tomb, so empty shall all the tombs of the world be when the archangel's trump shall sound. All hail, then, thou risen Jesus! Thou art he who once was dead, but who now liveth for evermore. At thy girdle are the keys of death and hell. March forward, thou mighty Conqueror in thy sublime victory! Let all the bells of heaven ring on this glad Easter morning! With thee we bare the cross; with thee we shall be buried in the grave; with thee we shall rise in triumph; and with thee we shall sit on thy throne to die no more, but to rejoice forever in the triumphs thou hast won—thou Christ of God, blessed for evermore!

XVIII.

𝔦ntercessory prayer and 𝔅eatific 𝔅ision.

"Father, I will that they also, whom thou hast given me, be with me where I am; that they may behold my glory, which thou hast given me : for thou lovedst me before the foundation of the world.—JOHN xvii. 24.

THE chapter from which this text is taken is one of the most beautiful and sacred portions of Holy Scripture. It is the Holy of Holies in the glorious Temple of Revelation. It consists of our Lord's intercessory prayer, the true Lord's Prayer. In this prayer the divine Redeemer anticipates his great sacrifice for human guilt, and on the ground of that sacrifice he offers this prayer for his chosen people. His thoughts are now to a great degree withdrawn from the world; already he seems to have entered into the closest communion with the Father; he speaks, indeed, as if his earthly work of suffering and sacrifice were already completed. This prayer followed immediately on the close of the discourse given in the previous chapter. Dr. Owen and others express the opinion that this prayer could scarcely have been offered on the way from the city to the Garden of Gethsemane. One feels in reading these calm and sublime utterances that they must have been spoken in some secluded place. It certainly seems unlikely that they could have been spoken on a great thoroughfare, which even at midnight, during Passover week, would be filled with the strangers then in and about Jerusalem. It is most natural to suppose that this prayer was uttered before Christ and the disciples left the supper-room. At the end of the 14th chapter we have read the words, " Arise, let us go hence;" but it seems more probable that although they arose to go, they still lingered around the table, unwilling to break off a discourse so sweet and heavenly. We can readily understand that all that is recorded in the 15th, 16th, and 17th chapters was spoken in the guest-chamber while the disciples stood about the Master. It is difficult to imagine that our Lord would have uttered these solemn, confidential, and sublime words on the street. He could not have spoken to eleven men, making a hasty departure from the city, without speaking in a comparatively loud tone; and such a tone would have been inconsistent with the thoughts expressed, and would also have exposed him and his disciples to danger from their foes. When both the discourse and the prayer were ended we can well believe that then they chanted the appropriate psalm and went forth into the Garden in solemn silence.

This is rightly called an intercessory prayer, and yet the term in this connection must have a special meaning. This is not the prayer of an inferior to a superior; it is rather the expression of the will of one who is conscious of equality with him to whom the expression is made. It gives us an illustration of the prayer of our great High Priest now before the throne. All commentators, ancient and modern, have spoken of the fact that the words of this prayer flow . on in equal simplicity and sublimity. The words themselves are so plain that the simplest minds may understand them; and yet they are so deep that no finite mind can sound all their meaning. Bengel says: "This chapter is the most easy in respect to its language and the most profound in respect to its sentiments." When John Knox came to die, he asked for the reading of this precious chapter. We are told that the devout Spener had it read to him three times when he was on his death-bed. Luther, Tholuck, Olshausen, Stier, Melanchthon and others speak of the profound impression which this high-priestly prayer made upon their minds and hearts. They confess their inability to scale its lofty heights, or to sound its profound depths.

The prayer has been variously divided. We may say that it consists of three main parts. In the first five verses we have the prayer for the glorification of the Son; in verses six to nineteen, intercession for his own, whom he leaves in the world, and beginning with the 20th verse and going to the end of the chapter we have a petition with largest range of meaning for the whole Church of God in all times. We may express the thought more briefly by saying that in the first division we have Christ's prayer for himself primarily; in the second for the apostles specifically, and in the third for believers generally. In studying the text it seemed fitting to say this much about the relation of the chapter to the discourse which preceded it, and on the prayer as a whole.

1. Let us notice, in the first place, the Petitioner. Here our Lord appears with kingly authority blending with priestly intercession. The words " I will " do not so much express increased earnestness as they suggest the Petitioner's essential and conscious equality with the Father. Who is this sublime Petitioner? Is he a man? Did man ever so address God? Did man ever venture to use language of such authority in his approaches to the Deity? This prayer is founded on the conscious right of the Petitioner to present this claim. He recognizes his relationship to the Eternal, his equality with Deity.

It is not so much a petition asking for a favor as it is a declaration of a purpose. He, as a king, expresses the purpose that those who are his should

share with him in his glory. If this be the language
of a mere man he must be a deeply sinful, a hope-
lessly presumptuous, a sadly blasphemous man. No
Old Testament saint ever so addressed God; Abraham did not so presume in the divine presence; in
that presence he spoke of himself as dust and ashes.
David did not so presume. Here is a voice conscious
of authority not possessed by patriarch or prophet,
not by psalmist or apostle. This utterance illustrates
the majesty of a sovereign rather than the humility of a subject. These are truly wonderful words.
Dare angel or archangel so pray? They prostrate
themselves before God and cry, "Holy, Holy, Holy,
Lord God of Hosts." This petition clearly implies
that Christ is equal to God, that he is God. At the
same time the prayer reveals his true humanity.
Here the divine and human graciously and wonderfully blend; but no skill of man can separate them
so as to describe what belongs to the human and
what to the divine. This Petitioner is the divine
Lord, holding sublime and ineffable communion with
his Father. We cannot but feel that here we are
standing on holy ground; that here we are in the
inner sanctuary, the Holy of Holies, of gospel history
and of divine revelation. We rightly say that the
will of the Son and the will of the Father are one;
that there is no collision, no contradiction, no contrast. The prayer of the Son, therefore, is the echo of

the desire of the Father; the Son's matchless words voiced the Father's eternal love and purpose. Christ is the Word. In him the Father's thought of love finds voice. If we know the Son we know the Father.

2. In studying this prayer we have, in the next place, its subjects, "they also whom thou hast given me." The objects of the Father's love were given to Christ, and are now the subjects of his petition. The reference is not to the apostles alone, but to believers in all times and places. Believers in Christ are given to him as the Father's most precious gift; and their love to Christ as his most resplendent jewel. There is unspeakable sweetness to every Christian heart in this divine relationship. All who are to be saved are given to Christ in the eternal purpose of God. No one but God knows who these are, but it is certain that they will be a vast number. The glowing prophecy of Isaiah teaches us that the Lord shall see of the travail of his soul and shall be satisfied. The description of heaven given in the Book of Revelation shows that the number of the redeemed will be unspeakably great. It will also be of all nations, kindreds, tongues, and people. Perhaps the number of the lost will be to the saved in some such proportion as the number now confined in prisons is to those at liberty in all the walks of life.

No question can be more important than this one, "Have we been given to Christ?" Are we clothed in his righteousness, washed in his blood, transformed into his likeness? How can any man know that he has been given thus to Christ? We cannot look into God's secret book; no angel can descend from heaven to make to us announcement regarding this matter. But still a man may know whether or not he is elected to be saved. The answer to the preplexing question is not to be found by inquisitive looking into God's secret counsels; it is not to be found in the indulgence of wicked presumption; it is not to be found in the culpable indifference which says, If I am to be saved, I shall be; if not, I cannot be. If a man will stop there, he certainly never will be saved. How then can we know that we have been given to Christ? The answer is simple and practical; every essential religious duty is simple and practical. As many are given to Christ by God as have given themselves to God through Christ; as many are elected to be saved as have elected Christ as their Saviour. A man knows that he is elected of God when God is elected by him. We may learn the answer to this great question just as we learn whether or not we are Christians. Your answers to the questions which I now ask will be answers to the questions which I have just asked: "Have you believed on Jesus Christ? Have you accepted him as your only Saviour? Have you committed your soul to his keeping? Can you say now that you trust him and him alone as your Saviour in life, in death, and in eternity? Do you answer me humbly but earnestly in the affirmative? Then you are of the number spoken of in this prayer. The question with us is not one of election on God's part so much as it is one of candidacy on our part, for no man is ever elected except he be a candidate. Are you with all your soul a candidate? Then, as God liveth, you are elected to eternal salvation. If we have committed our souls to Christ it is as certain that God has committed us to him as if an angel from heaven should announce that fact by an audible voice at this moment. The committal of our souls to Christ is just the earthly side of God's eternal committal of our souls to Christ. If you choose God in Christ you have the best and only evidence possible that God has chosen you in Christ. If you are excluded from those for whom Christ prayed it is because you exclude yourself. If you are not with Christ now in love and faith you cannot be with Christ at last in his glory. Oh, give yourself to-day to the Lord Jesus, and you shall have the blessed evidence that you have been given to him by God as his most precious gift. Commit yourself to his keeping now, and you shall know that he will keep you as his choicest treasure until that day when he shall make up his jewels.

3. Notice, in the third place, the petition itself— that they may " be with me where I am; that they

17

may behold my glory, which thou hast given me."
The first thought in this prayer is that Christ's own
may be with him. These are wonderful words.
They are high; we cannot attain to them. They are
deep; we cannot fathom them. There is here an
outpouring of Christ's eternal love. The thought
cannot be comprehended, far less expressed. This
great honor is the result of his great love. It would
be false humility which would lead us to refuse what
that love bestows. True humility is seen in doing,
being, and having what his grace gives. This
prayer of Christ is very precious; he would have us
where he is. Christ's presence is heaven. Anywhere with Jesus is heaven; nowhere without him
can his disciples have heaven. Here our Lord con-
ceives of himself as already having finished his life,
completed his sacrifice, and returned to his Father.
He, therefore, presents this claim for the eternal
companionship of his disciples. They, like him, are
to pass from earthly toil to heavenly glory. His
thoughts sweep past the cross and the tomb to the
crown and the throne. This part of the petition is
in harmony with the sentiment expressed in the
second and third verses of the fourteenth chapter,
where he speaks of his Father's house and the place
he was going to prepare. We behold here the matchless mystery of eternal and ineffable love. Christ
longs for our presence; our companionship is sweet

to him. It would seem as if heaven would be incomplete to him without the presence of his redeemed. This is marvellous condescension on his part; this is indescribable exaltation for us. Such condescending love is like Christ. We are to be with him, and that not at his feet, but on his throne. As he overcame and is enthroned, so we are to overcome and be enthroned by his side. Further he could not go. Additional exaltation is impossible.

We learn also that we are to behold his glory. While he was upon earth that glory was obscured; to become man he veiled its splendor. Its brightness would dazzle and blind our human eyes. During his earthly life the hidden glory once burst through the veil of flesh, and the disciples were overwhelmed with its splendor. Now we have eyes to see only through a glass darkly; now we have minds able to know only in part; but the life to come shall give us the beatific vision of our Lord. We shall then see the King in his beauty. Many passages of Scripture fully corroborate these statements. The word here translated "behold" implies the open sight of his glory; and it suggests our transformation into his perfect image. He so loved his people that he came to die for them; he so loves them still that he desires them to reign with him forever. He is the head; they are the members of his body. Only when they are together will the glory of both be complete. The

exalted occupation of the redeemed will be in beholding the glory of the Redeemer. Probably the glory
here meant is that for which he prayed when he said,
" Glorify thou me, with thine own self, with the glory
which I had with thee before the world was."
Earlier in his prayer we see his longing to be at the
Father's side; now we see his longing to have his
saints at his side. We are to be like Christ, because
we shall see him as he is; and it is also true that we
shall see him as he is because we shall be like him.
These two truths cannot be separated. This glory
would then include the whole sweep of his eternal
perfections and character. Moses prayed, "Show
me thy glory," and God made all his goodness pass
before him. There is material in this part of my
text for a volume. We may say with Dr. Cumming,
that we shall behold his creative glory, his providential glory, and, most of all, his redemptive glory.
This latter is the grandest thought of heaven. To
see this glory the angels had strong desire. We already know something of its mystery and majesty;
already some drops of the divine love have come into
our hearts; but in heaven we shall bathe in an ocean
of love. Then we shall know the preciousness of
that blood which hath cleansed us; then we shall
know the excellence of that righteousness whose robe
we wear; then we shall know something of the
breadth, height, and depth of that love which passeth

all knowledge. Blessed knowledge! Glorious day!
Beatific vision! May the prayer of Christ be answered in the experience of us all.

4. We notice, in the last place, the ground or argument for this petition—"for thou lovedst me before
the foundation of the world." This, at first sight,
seems to be strange language. I confess that in studying this passage I did not at once see its relation to
the previous parts of the text; but when I did its
meaning was to me unspeakably glorious. We see
here that the Father's love is the reason for giving
the Son such wonderful glory as that already described. Had the words been, "for thou lovedst them
before the foundation of the world" the meaning
would seem more apparent. That also is true, for
God did so love men. But to understand this great
thought we must go deeper into the mystery and
beauty of Christ's rhetoric. The ground of our hope
is not merely God's love to us, but God's love to
Christ. The glory promised is not due to any arbitrary allotment or capricious arrangement. Christ
and his people are one; he is in them and they in
him, but we advance a step; not only are we Christ's
but Christ is God's. God sees his people in his only-
begotten and well-beloved Son. God's love to Christ
antedates the creation of all human beings. It was
a love which existed from eternity between the persons of the blessed Godhead. When we are in Christ

by faith we share in the Father's love for the divine Son. When Christ's work is completed, he will present us as a glorious people without spot or wrinkle or any such thing. Luther said of this text, "We should make this sentence our pillow, and a bed of down for our souls, and with a glad heart repair to it when the happy hour draws nigh." My highest wish for you, my dear hearers, and for myself, is expressed by the apostle Paul when he said of himself: "And be found in him, not having mine own righteousness, which is of the law, but that which is through the faith of Christ, the righteousness which is of God by faith." If you have given your hearts unto Christ then God has given you unto Christ; then you are prayed for in this text; then you shall be with him where he is; then you shall behold his glory, and then you may go on developing in knowledge and character, gazing upon this beatific vision, and so finish this sermon in heaven.